One Way Back to Me

A Wilder Brothers Novel

Carrie Ann Ryan

ONE WAY BACK TO ME

A WILDER BROTHERS NOVEL

By
Carrie Ann Ryan

One Way Back to Me
A Wilder Brothers Love
By: Carrie Ann Ryan
© 2022 Carrie Ann Ryan
eBook 978-1-950443-74-1
Paperback 978-1-950443-75-8

Cover Art by Sweet N Spicy Designs

Praise for Carrie Ann Ryan

"Count on Carrie Ann Ryan for emotional, sexy, character driven stories that capture your heart!" – Carly Phillips, NY Times bestselling author

"Carrie Ann Ryan's romances are my newest addiction! The emotion in her books captures me from the very beginning. The hope and healing hold me close until the end. These love stories will simply sweep you away." ~ NYT Bestselling Author Deveny Perry

"Carrie Ann Ryan writes the perfect balance of sweet and heat ensuring every story feeds the soul." - Audrey Carlan, #1 New York Times Bestselling Author

"Carrie Ann Ryan never fails to draw readers in with passion, raw sensuality, and characters that pop off the page. Any book by Carrie Ann is an absolute treat." – New York Times Bestselling Author J. Kenner

"Carrie Ann Ryan knows how to pull your heartstrings and make your pulse pound! Her wonderful Redwood Pack series will draw you in and keep you reading long into the night. I can't wait to see what comes next with the new generation, the Talons. Keep them coming, Carrie Ann!" –Lara Adrian, New York Times bestselling author of CRAVE THE NIGHT

"With snarky humor, sizzling love scenes, and brilliant, imaginative worldbuilding, The Dante's Circle series reads as if Carrie Ann Ryan peeked at my personal wish list!" – NYT Bestselling Author, Larissa Ione

"Carrie Ann Ryan writes sexy shifters in a world full of passionate happily-ever-afters." – *New York Times* Bestselling Author Vivian Arend

"Carrie Ann's books are sexy with characters you can't help but love from page one. They are heat and heart blended to perfection." *New York Times* Bestselling Author Jayne Rylon

Carrie Ann Ryan's books are wickedly funny and deliciously hot, with plenty of twists to keep you guessing. They'll keep you up all night!" USA Today Bestselling Author Cari Quinn

"Once again, Carrie Ann Ryan knocks the Dante's Circle series out of the park. The queen of hot, sexy, enthralling paranormal romance, Carrie Ann is an author not to miss!" *New York Times* bestselling Author Marie Harte

One Way Back to Me

The Wilder brothers have retired from the military and as they're forced to learn a new life, things get interesting fast in this kickoff to a brand new steamy, contemporary romance series from NYT Bestselling Author Carrie Ann Ryan.

One dance at a stranger's wedding. That's all it took for me to fall for Alexis.

And then? Disaster. Another man—her boyfriend—gets down on one knee and proposes to her.

I never thought I'd see her again.

Years later, I'm in desperate need of a wedding planner—not for myself, but for my company.

My five brothers and I need to get our new Wilder

Resort off the ground, and Alexis is the only one savvy enough to help us.

But there's the little matter that I still have it bad for her. Alexis has changed since the night we met. She's gun shy. But there's a spark between us that will not die. We both fight it, until we don't.

Until history repeats itself. The same guy who took her away from me is back to do more damage. But this time he'll have to go through me to get her.

Chapter One

Eli

When my morning begins with me standing ankle-deep in a basement full of water, I know I probably should have stayed in bed. Only, I was the boss, and I didn't get that choice.

"Hold on. I'm looking for it." East cursed underneath his breath as my younger brother bent down around the pipe, trying his best to turn off the valve. I sighed, waded through the muck in my work boots, and moved to help him. "I said I've got it," East snapped, but I ignored him.

I narrowed my eyes at the evil pipe. "It's old and rusted, and even though it passed an inspection over a year ago, we knew this was going to be a problem."

"And I'm the fucking handyman of this company. I've got this."

"And as a handyman, you need a hand."

"You're hilarious. Seriously. I don't know how I could ever manage without your wit and humor." The dryness in his tone made my lips twitch even as I did my best to ignore the smell of whatever water we stood in.

"Fuck you," I growled.

"No thanks. I'm a little too busy for that."

With a grunt, East shut off the water, and we both stood back, hands on our hips as we stared at the mess of this basement.

East let out a sigh. "I'm not going to have to turn the water off for the whole property, but I'm glad that we don't have tenants in this particular cabin."

I nodded tightly and held back a sigh. "This is probably why there aren't basements in Texas. Because everything seems to go wrong in these things."

"I'm pretty sure this is a storm shelter, or at least a tornado one. Not quite sure as it's one of the only basements in the area."

"It was probably the only one that they had the

energy to make back in the day. Considering this whole place is built over clay and limestone."

East nodded, looked around. "I'll start the cleanup with this water, and we'll look to see what we can do with the pipes."

I pinched the bridge of my nose. "I don't want to have to replace the plumbing for this whole place."

"At least it's not the villa itself, or the farmhouse, or the winery. Just a single cabin."

I glared at my younger brother, then reached out and knocked on a wooden pillar. "Shut your mouth. Don't say things like that to me. We are just now getting our feet under us."

East shrugged. "It's the truth, though. However much you weigh it, it could have been worse."

I pinched the bridge of my nose. "Jesus Christ. You were in the military for how long? A Wilder your entire life, and you say things like that? When the hell did you lose that superstition bone?"

"About the time that my Humvee was blown up, and when Evan's was, Everett's too. Hell, about the time that you almost fell out of the sky in your plane. Or when Elliot was nearly shot to death trying to help one of his men. So, yes, I pretty much lost all superstition when trying to toe the line ended up in near death and maiming."

I met my brother's gaze, that familiar pang thinking about all that we had lost and almost lost over the past few years.

East muttered under his breath, shaking his head. "And I sound more and more like Evan these days rather than myself."

I squeezed his shoulder and let out a breath, thinking of our brother who grunted more that spoke these days. "It's okay. We've been through a lot. But we're here."

Somehow, we were here. I wasn't quite sure if we had made the right decision about two years ago when we had formed this plan, or rather *I* had formed this plan, but there was no going back. We were in it, and we were going to have to find a way to make it work, flooded former tornado shelters and all.

Evan sighed. "I'll work on this now. Then I'll head on over to the main house. I have a few things to work on there."

"You know, we can hire you help. I know we had all the contractors and everything to work with us for some of the rebuilds and rehabs, but we can hire someone else for you on a day-to-day basis."

My brother shook his head. "We may be able to afford it, but I'd rather save that for a rainy day. Because when it rains, it pours here, and flash flooding is a major threat in this part of Texas." He winked as he said it, mixing his metaphors, and I just shook my head.

"You just let me know if you need it."

"You're the CEO, brother of mine, not the CFO. That's Everett."

"True, but we did talk about it so we can work on it." I paused, thinking about what other expenses might show up. "And what do you need to do with the villa?"

The villa was the main house where most things happened on the property. It contained the lobby, library, and atrium. My apartment was also on the top floor, so I could be there for emergencies. Our innkeeper lived on the other side of the house, but I was in the main loft because this was my project, my baby.

My other brothers, all five of them, lived in cabins on the property. We lived together, worked together, ate together, and fought together. We were the Wilder brothers. It was what we did.

I had left to join the Air Force at seventeen, having graduated early, leaving behind my kid brothers and sister. After nearly twenty years of doing what we needed to in order to survive, we hadn't spent as much time with one another as I would have like. We hadn't been stationed together, so we hadn't seen one another for longer than holidays or in passing.

But now we were together. At least most of us. So I was going to make this work, even if it killed me.

East finally answered my question. "I just have to fix a door that's a little too squeaky in one of the guestrooms. Not a big deal."

I raised a brow. "That's it?"

"It's one of the many things on my list. Thankfully, this place is big enough that I always have something to do. It's an unending list. And that the winery has its own team to work on all of that shit, because I'm not in the mood to learn to deal with any of the complicated machinery that comes with that world."

I snorted. "Honestly, same. I'm glad there are people that know what the fuck they're doing when it comes to wine making so that didn't have to be the two of us."

I left my brother to this job, knowing he liked time on his own, just like the rest of us did, and went to dry my boots. I was working by myself for most of the day, in interviews and other "boss business," as Elliot called it, so I had to focus and get clean.

I wasn't in the mood to deal with interviews, but it was part of my job. We had to fill positions that hadn't been working out over the past year, some more than others.

Wilder Retreat was a place that hadn't been even a spark in my mind my entire life. No, I had been too busy being a career military man—getting in my twenty, moving up the ranks, and ending up as a Lieutenant Colonel before I got out. I had been a commander of a squadron, and yet, it felt like I didn't know how to command where I was now.

When my sister Eliza had lost her husband when he was on deployment, it had been the last domino to fall in the Wilder brothers' military career. I had been ready to get out with twenty years in, knowing I needed a career outside of being a Lieutenant Colonel. I wasn't even forty yet, and the term retirement was a misnomer, but that's what happened when it came to my former job.

East had been getting out around that time for reasons of his own, and then Evan had been forced to. I rubbed my hand over my chest, that familiar pain, remembering the phone call from one of Evan's commanders when Evan had been hurt.

I thought I'd lost my baby brother then, and we nearly had. Everett had gotten hurt too, and Elijah and Elliot had needed out for their own reasons. Losing our baby sister's husband had just pushed us forward.

Finding out that Eliza's husband had been a cheating asshole had just cemented the fact that we needed to spend more time together as a family so we could be there for one another.

In retrospect, it would have been nice if Eliza would

have been able to come down to Texas with us, to our suburb outside of San Antonio. Only, she had fallen in love again, with a man with a big family and a good heart up in Fort Collins, Colorado. She was still up there and traveled down enough that we actually got to get to know our sister again.

It was weird to think that, after so many years of always seeing each other in passing or through video calls, most of us were here, opening up a business. And all because I had been losing my mind.

Wilder Retreat and Winery was a villa and wedding venue outside of San Antonio. We were in hill country, at least what passed for hill country in South Texas, and the place had been owned by a former Air Force General who had wanted to retire and sell the place, since his kid didn't want it.

It was a large spread that used to be a ranch back in the day, nearly one hundred acres that the original owners had taken from a working ranch, and instead of making it a dude ranch or something similar, like others did around here, they'd added a winery using local help. We were close enough to Fredericksburg that it made sense in terms of the soil and weather. They had been able to add on additions, so it wasn't just the winery. Someone could come for the day for a winery tour or even a retreat tour, but most people came for the weekend or for a whole week. There were cabins and a farmhouse where we held weddings, dances, or other events. We had some chickens and ducks that gave us eggs, and goats that seemed to have a mind of their own and provided milk for cheese. Then there was the main annex, which housed all the equipment for the retreat villa.

The winery had its own section of buildings, and it was far bigger than anything I would have ever thought that we could handle. But, between the six of us, we did.

And the only reason we could even afford it, because one didn't afford something like this on a military salary, even with a decent retirement plan, was because of our uncles.

Our uncles, Edward and Edmond Wilder, had owned Wilder Wines down in Napa, California, for years. They had done well for themselves, and when we had been kids, we had gone out to visit. Evan had been the one that had clung to it and had been interested in wine making before he had changed his mind and gone into the military like the rest of us.

That was why Evan was in charge of the winery itself now. Because he knew what he was doing, even if he'd growled and said he didn't. Either way though, the place was huge, had multiple working parts at all times, and we had a staff that needed us. But when the uncles had died, they had left any money from the sale of the winery to us in equal parts. Eliza had taken hers to invest for her future children, and the rest of us had pooled our money together to buy this place and make it ours. A lot of the staff from the old owner had stayed, but some had left as well. Because they didn't want new owners who had no idea what they were doing, or they just retired. Either way, we were over a year in and doing okay.

Except for two positions that made me want to groan.

I had an interview with who would be our third wedding planner since we started this. The main proponent of the retreat was to have an actual wedding venue. To be able to host parties, and not just wine tours. Elliot was our major event planner that helped with our yearly and seasonal minute details, but he didn't want anything to do with the actual weddings. That was a whole other skill set, and so we wanted a wedding planner. We had gone through two wedding planners now, and we needed to hire a third. The first one had lied on her résumé, had given references that were her friends who had lied and had even created websites that were all fabrication, all so she could get into the business. Which, I understood, getting into the business is one thing. However, lying was another. Plus, we needed someone with actual experience because we didn't have any ourselves. We were going out on a limb here with this whole retreat business, and it was all because I had the harebrained idea of getting our family to work together, get along, and get to know one another. I wanted us to have a future, to be our own bosses.

And it was so far over my head that I knew that if I didn't get reliable help, we were going to fail.

Later, I had a meeting with that potential wedding planner. But first, I had to see what the fuck that smell was coming from the main kitchen in the villa.

The second wedding planner we hired was a guy with great and *true* references, one who was good at his job but hated everything to do with my brothers and me. He had hated the idea of the retreat and how rustic it was, even though we were in fucking South Texas. Yes, the buildings look slightly European because that was the theme that the original owners had gone for. Still, the guy had hated us, hadn't listened to us, and had called us white trash before he had walked away, jumped into his convertible, and sped off down the road, leaving us without help. He had been rude to our guests, and now Elliot was the one having to plan weddings for the past three weeks. My brother was going to strangle me soon if we didn't hire someone. And this person was going to be our last hope. As soon as she showed up, that was.

I looked down on my watch and tried to plan the rest of my day. I had thirty minutes to figure out what the hell was going on in the kitchen, and then I had to go to the meeting.

I nodded at a few guests who were sipping wine and eating a cheese plate and then at our innkeeper, Naomi. Naomi's honey-brown hair was cut in an angled bob that lit her face, and she grinned at me.

"Hello there, Boss Man," she whispered. "You might need to go to the kitchen."

"Do I want to know?" I asked with a grumble.

"I'm not sure. But I am going to go check in our next guest, and then Elliott needs to meet with the Henderson couple."

"He'll be there." I didn't say that Elliot would rather chew off his own arm rather than deal with this, considering we had a family event coming in, one that Elliot was on target with planning. The wedding for next year was an important one, so we needed to work on it.

Naomi was a fantastic innkeeper, far more organized in any of us—and that was saying something since my brothers and I knew our way around schedules, to-do lists, and spreadsheets. Naomi was personable, smiled, and kept us on our toes.

Without her, I knew we wouldn't be able to do this. Hell, without Amos, our vineyard manager, I knew that Evan and Elijah wouldn't be able to handle the winery as they did. Naomi and Amos had come with the place when we had bought it, and I would be forever grateful that they had decided to stay on.

I gave Naomi another nod, then headed back to the kitchen and nearly walked right back out.

Tony stood there, a scowl on his face and his hands on his hips. "I don't understand what the fuck is wrong with this oven."

"What's going on?" I asked as Everett stood by Tony. Everett was my quiet brother with usually a small smile on his face, only right then it looked like he was ready to scream.

I didn't know why Everett was even there since he was part responsible for the financials side of the company and usually worked with Elliot these days. Maybe he had come to the kitchen after the smell of burning as I had after Naomi's prodding.

Tony threw his hands in the air. "What's going on? This stove is a piece of shit. All of it is a piece of shit. I'm tired of this rustic place. I thought I would be coming to a Michelin star restaurant. To be my own chef. Instead, I have to make English breakfasts and pancakes with bananas. I might as well be at a bed and breakfast."

I pinched the bridge of my nose. "We're an inn, not a bed and breakfast."

"But I serve breakfast. That's all I do these days. That and cheese platters. Nobody comes for dinner. Nobody comes for lunch."

That was a lie. Tony worked for the winery and the retreat itself and served all the meals. But Tony wanted to go crazy with the menu, to try new and fantastical items that just weren't going to work here.

And I had a feeling I was going to throw up if I wasn't careful.

"I quit," Tony snapped, and I knew right then, it was done for. I was done.

"You can't quit," I growled while Everett held back a sigh.

"Yes, I can. I'm done. I'm done with you and this ranch. You're not cowboys. You're not even Texans. You're just people moving in on our territory." And with that, Tony stomped away, throwing his chef's apron on the ground.

I was thankful that the kitchen was on the other side of the library and front area, where most of the guests were if they weren't out on one of the tours of the area and city that Elliott had arranged for them. That was the whole point of this retreat. They could come visit, and could relax, or we could set them up on a tour of downtown San Antonio, or Canyon Lake, or any of the other places that were nearby.

And yet, Tony had just thrown a wrench into all of that. I didn't know what was worse, the smell of burning, Tony leaving, the water in the basement that wasn't truly a basement, or the fact that I was going to smell like charred food and wet jeans when I went to go meet this wedding planner.

"You're going to need to hire a new cook," Everett whispered.

I looked at my brother, at the man who did his best to make sure we didn't go bankrupt, and I wanted to just grumble. "I figured."

"I can help for now, but you know I'm only part-time. I can't stay away from my twins for too long," Sandy said as she came forward to take the pan off the stove. "I wish I could do full time, but this is all I can do for now."

Sandy had come back from maternity leave after we had already opened the retreat. She had been on with the former owners and was brilliant. But she had a right to be a mom and not want to work full time. I understood that, and I knew that Sandy didn't want to handle a whole kitchen by herself. She liked her position as a sous chef.

I was going to have to figure out what to do. Again.

"I'll get it done," I said while rubbing my temples.

"You know what we need to do," Everett whispered, and I shook my head.

"He'll kill us."

"Maybe, but it'll be worth it in the end. And speaking of, don't you have that interview soon? Or do you want me to take it?" His gaze tracked to my jeans.

I shook my head. "No, help Sandy."

Everett winced. "Just because I know how to slice an onion, it doesn't mean I'm good at cooking."

"I'm sorry, did you just say you could slice an onion? Get to it," Sandy put in with a smile, pointing at the sink. "Wash those hands."

"I cannot believe I just said that out loud. I just stepped right into it," Everett said with a sigh. "Go to the interview. You know what to ask."

"I do. And I hope we don't get screwed this time."

"You know, if we're lucky, we'll get someone as good as Roy's wedding planner, or at least that woman that we met. You know who she is." Everett grinned like a cat with the canary.

I narrowed my eyes. "Don't bring her up."

"Oh, I can't help it. A single dance, and you were drawn to her."

"What dance? You know what? No, I don't have

time. We have to work on lunch and dinner. Tell me while you work," Sandy added with a wink.

Everett leaned toward her as he washed his hands. "Well, you see, there was this dance, and he met the perfect woman, and then she got engaged."

Sandy's eyes widened. "Engaged? How did that happen? She was dating someone else?" she asked as she looked at me.

I pinched the bridge of my nose. "It was at Roy's place when we were looking at the venue to see if we wanted to buy the retreat here." I sighed, I knew if I just let it all out, she would move on from this conversation, and I would never have to deal with it again. "Somehow, I ended up at a wedding there, caught the garter. This woman caught the bouquet, and she happened to be the wedding planner. We danced, we laughed, and as she walked away, her boyfriend got down on one knee and proposed."

"No way!" She leaned forward with a fierce look on her face, her eyes bright. "What did she say?"

"I have no clue. I left." I ignored whatever feeling might want to show up at that thought. Everett gave me a glance, and I shook my head. "Enough of that. Yes, the wedding that she did was great, but I honestly have no idea who she is, and she has a job. She doesn't need to work here." And I didn't know what I would do if I saw her again or had to work with her. There had been such an intense connection that I knew it would be awkward as hell. But thankfully, she had her own business and wasn't going to come to the Wilder Retreat for a job.

I left Sandy and Everett on their own, knowing that they were capable, at least for now. And I knew who we would have to hire if she said yes, and if my other brother didn't kill me first.

I washed my hands in the sink on the way out, grateful that at least I looked somewhat decent, if not a little disheveled, and made my way out front, hoping that the wedding planner who came in through the doors would be the one that would stick. Because we needed some good luck. After the day we've had, we needed some good luck.

I turned the corner and nearly tripped over my feet.

Because, of course, fate was this way.

It was her.

Of all the wedding planners from all the wedding venues, it was her.

Chapter Two

Alexis

This wasn't what I expected my life to be, but then again, what had I expected?

Marriage, kids, a fruitful career, a business that I loved, and a plan. All of that had been a decent dream. One I thought maybe I could bring to fruition.

Then the world remembered I was Alexis Lane, and I didn't get that kind of happiness.

As I drove down the highway, my hands tightened on the steering wheel and I took the next exit, towards the Wilder Retreat and Winery. This was my last shot.

At least in this area of Texas. If this didn't work, if I had to find another job, it would have to be in another area. I would have to start my business over from scratch, without what few contacts I had left, without my place, and not in the San Antonio or Austin areas. The I-35 corridor would be forever dead to me. And it was my own damn fault.

I turned down the next major street, ignoring the traffic and the Texas drivers—who didn't honk but did glare at you from their large trucks. I did my best to just focus on what I could. The fact that I was indeed on my last straw. My last chance.

I didn't have another chance in me.

I took another right at the light and focused on my surroundings, on the beautiful oak and cedar trees that were well aged and rooted. There were no new developments out here, just one-hundred-year-old oaks that reached to the sky—and hurt my allergies, but that's what allergy pills were for. The trees were gorgeous and would be all year, and my allergies would just have to deal. They always did.

I pulled off onto not precisely a dirt road but a minor farm road and kept going, letting the GPS find my way. I went through my list of everything that I knew about the Wilder Resort and Winery. It was a little over a year old, a family-run business, and from what I heard, they were great at what they did but needed help in the wedding planning department. Their other events and parties seemed to go off well. Though there were probably a few hitches with any young business, they were hard workers. At least that's what Roy told me.

Roy. A man who gave me my second and third chance. But he already had a full-time wedding planner, and it hadn't been me. Not from my own mistakes. No, from Clint's.

I ground my teeth and told myself not to think about him. He didn't have any place here, even if he was the whole reason I was doing this.

Back to the Wilders. They had no experience in this area, and I had no idea if they knew what they were doing, considering the place also had a damn winery attached to it, but that would be great for weddings, just like Roy had the brewery. It was a good idea, and they seemed to be steady. But I didn't want steady. I didn't want to flounder. I wanted to *thrive*. I wanted *them* to thrive.

For that to happen, I needed the job.

And I had to hope that I was enough.

I turned onto the ranch's main road and sucked in a breath, a smile threatening even as the stress took over.

The place was *gorgeous*. There were rolling hills behind the main drag of trees. I could see smaller cabins off to the side, some tucked behind bigger trees, but everything was well kept, the grounds gorgeous, just not manicured. And that was the point. We were on a Texas retreat and ranch, it wasn't going to be precisely manicured, but it would be well taken care of.

The wrought iron gates that proclaimed the Wilder Retreat looked new, and signs directed people to the welcome area, the villa, the wedding venue, and the winery. I wanted to visit all of it, but first, I needed to go to the main house and meet with this Eli Wilder.

I needed this job. No matter what happened next, I needed this job. And I needed Eli Wilder to hire me and for things to make sense.

I did not want to move. I did not want to start over once again. Even though I was starting over now, it wasn't by choice.

And this place already called to me. As I pulled into the front area I gasped, my hands tightening around the steering wheel. The place was beautiful.

There were two large buildings in the center, with paths to other small buildings around, but the majesty of what lay before me left me breathless.

According to their website, there was the main villa to the left, where I knew most of the rooms had to be, but attached to it with an open walkway was the welcome center, which also had a circular driveway to get to the winery.

Everything looked based on European architecture, but not German as was typical around this area. It looked as if someone had taken their favorite parts of certain architecture and pieced them together, and I knew it had to do with the original owners and not the Wilders, but I loved what the Wilders had now.

I stepped out of the car, grateful that the ground was paved and not gravel, since I was wearing my tall heels that made my legs look great and gave me the confidence I needed today.

The buildings in front of me were a white stone and stucco, gorgeous and well kept. There were trees all around, but in the center in front of the parking area, and off to the side just slightly, were these square stone pavers that looked to be an art piece, and I knew would be gorgeous for bride photos or any party images. It was as if someone had wanted their own mosaic, but with a Texas twist, and I couldn't help but smile. Off to the side of that was a large open-sided farmhouse that was for events, and weddings could be performed in there, as well as the open archways in front of it. Everything looked relaxed, slightly Texan, slightly refined, and elegant.

People were milling about, looking happy, going

about their day. I saw gardeners and maids and other staff members moving, everyone smiling and getting along.

The only thing this place needed was a wedding planner.

And, hopefully, that could be me.

What was good about this position was that it also came with room and board. Considering I was currently sleeping on a friend's couch—a friend that needed me out since her husband was coming back stateside after being deployed for eight months—I needed this to happen.

I couldn't believe I had been so stupid with Clint that I had lost *everything*. But no longer. This would be all mine.

I grabbed my bag, rolled my shoulders back, and made my way inside the beautiful building. Everything inside shone brightly, with white stone and polished wood. It was slightly masculine, with feminine touches of floral arrangements and delicate decorations. It was a beautiful dichotomy, and I loved it.

I moved forward and nearly tripped over my feet, a familiar face I hadn't expected, but I should have, because I remembered that dance. I remembered Roy's smile as he had explained to me who I had danced with and why the other man had been at that wedding. The wedding that had changed everything. The wedding that had broken me before I had even realized it.

I knew this man.

We had only exchanged first names before, but I should have put it together.

The man I had danced with and had felt that spark of connection with—that I had dutifully ignored—had been Eli Wilder.

The man I needed to be my boss.

"You," he whispered, and I blinked, aware that there were others around, but they were all in their own world, happy, relaxed, and enjoying themselves, and they didn't pay attention to two people standing on the edge of a weary abyss.

I swallowed hard and smiled. "You," I said, knowing that if I pretended that I didn't recognize him, that would be starting off this business relationship with a lie. And considering we had already started off our business relationship with a dance with a bouquet and a garter attached, I didn't want this to be the end of it.

"Sorry, hi, I'm Eli Wilder, and you must be Alexis Lane."

I did my best not to teeter on my heels, a little nervous, and nodded. "I am. And it's good to see you again."

His eyes widened fractionally, and I was glad that I

hadn't lied, hadn't pretended that I didn't know him.

"I didn't know your name before, but I should have. Considering Roy sent over your resume."

My eyes widened. "I didn't realize he had done that. And, honestly, I should have known it was you. Although it's been two years, part of me had assumed that you'd already be settled."

He cringed, and I felt like a jerk. He just put me so off-kilter. "We are. Mostly. Just not with your position. It's a long story. We can talk it over if things go well."

I nodded and held out my hand. He shook it, and I ignored the tension, the heat, the firmness of his hand. His fingers were calloused, not soft, not a man who sat behind a desk often. He may be the CEO, but this was a family establishment, and I knew he had done something completely different before this.

And why was I so busy worrying about his hands? This could be my boss, for goodness' sake. I needed to be better than this.

Not paying attention to my business while living my life had gotten me into this problem.

"Anyway, let's talk."

I smiled wide, my knees threatening to shake. "Yes. I'd love to know what you are looking for and what I can do for you. And exactly what the job entails."

"We can do all of that. Do you want to sit in the

office? Or do you want a tour?"

I smiled, I couldn't help it. "I'd love a tour. From what I've seen, it's gorgeous. And I'm not just saying that because it's an interview."

He laughed, his eyes brightening, and I did my best not to pay attention to them. "I love the place too. It's why we bought it, taking the risk that we did."

"There sounds like there's a story." I wanted to know all of it, and that was probably a problem.

"There is, and I can tell you it. It's not a secret."

"Good. I'd like to know."

"We can put your bag in my office first, or behind the desk with Naomi." He waved at a woman with a pretty haircut and a bright smile.

The woman beamed. "I can watch it for you. I'll keep it safe. I promise."

"Naomi, this is Alexis, Alexis, Naomi."

"It's nice to meet you," I said as I handed over my bag.

"No worries. We'll keep it safe since it's my job, and if you have any questions while you're here, don't hesitate to ask."

"Will do, thank you."

She grinned, then mouthed over Eli's shoulder 'good luck,' and I held back a laugh. Everybody seemed friendly here, and I hoped that this worked out. Because it just felt right. And not just because this was my only option.

"Let's go. I'll show you around."

"The place is beautiful."

"The original owners kept up with it, at least with the main house and the villa. The farmhouse needed some upgrades, as do many of the cabins, but we're working on it."

"I read there were cabins, but I don't know how many."

"Twenty of them."

My eyes widened. "Twenty?"

He grinned then and I ignored the heat flaring in my belly. "It's big. Probably bigger than what we bargained for at first, but we're making it work."

"I'm sure you can fill the cabins if you do on-site weddings."

He smiled, and I tried not to stare. It wasn't easy. "That's the goal. And that means we need a wedding planner who can draw in business as much as the resort itself."

"I know the area, and the vendors, so yes, I hope so, too."

"Good, I talked to Roy about that. He's sorry that he hired someone already and is a little grumbly about it even though Samantha's perfect for him."

I held back a smile. "I was a little grumbly at first, too."

"Roy's been in the business longer. I get it. However, I'm not going to say that his loss hurts too much because it could be our gain. Anyway, the villa itself has ten rooms, while the attachments have our breakfast room, dining room, atrium, kitchen, library, and the innkeeper's room. My place is on the top floor as well."

I raised my brow. "Really?"

He cleared his throat. "I mean, not to tell you where I'm sleeping, just, you know, that we all live on site. I just happen to live in what we deemed the penthouse, though it's not as fancy as that."

I blinked, awkwardness settling in, but then we moved on and I was grateful.

We moved outside of the main structure, and he nodded over at the front circle. "The driveway, as you can see, surrounds our first fountain, we have a reflection pool and a few other places in the back that came with the property, and we're adding our own touches. Either way, though, weddings can be done on the pavers themselves, on the grasslands, underneath the overheads that we've made, or in the farmhouse. That's what they've always done, and we've had other events here that my brother Elliot works on."

I tried to take it all in and just stared at the beauty of

it and all the possibilities. This place was huge, yet the Wilder brothers seemed to be even bigger. "And Elliot doesn't do weddings."

"Elliot could if he wanted to, but he is already doing yearly and seasonal minute details and works with all of us. He and I do our best to keep the winery and the resort itself together. So that means he's doing the big picture stuff and knows someone who actually has experience as a wedding planner should be doing that part."

I nodded, a million different things running through my head at once. "And *not* because I'm a woman."

Eli raised a brow. "The wedding planner that we had before you was a man, and he did a fantastic job, until he didn't. So, no, it's not that, it's more than Elliot has his job and wedding planning isn't it. We need someone that can work with Elliot, and me, for that matter. You're going to have to work with all of my brothers."

"It is a family-run business." I smiled.

"All of us work here, have jobs, and do our best to work well. Our sister is up in Fort Collins; she's married and has a whole life and family up there, but she visits often and tries to run us ragged, even though she's the youngest."

"It sounds like an amazing family." I tried to ignore the wistfulness in my voice.

My heart hurt just a bit since I missed my family. They were so far away, having all moved to Spain to be with my brother's wife. When my brother had gotten married, it had been a beautiful occasion, and I had even planned the American ceremony, and then I had gone to Spain for the second ceremony, and my brother had stayed. And when he and his wife had had two kids, our retired parents had decided to move to Spain to be with them. They lived in the house to the left of my brother and sister-in-law and their family, while my sister-in-law's parents lived to the right. Everybody lived so close to one another. They were raising the next generation as a family, a unit.

And I had been left behind.

I ignored the pain in my heart at that, wondering why I was thinking about that at all.

Eli studied my face a moment before speaking. "Let's go over a few other things and show you around."

He showed me the rest of the property and we moved through the winery. I met a growling and brooding Evan who was the winemaking director, and while he didn't look like any winemaking director I'd ever met, he knew what the hell he was doing. At least from what I saw from a distance.

Everybody had a place, and I was never going to

remember their names, but I would do my best because I wanted this job. I needed it.

We moved back into the main building, and I took my bag back from a smiling Naomi before she went to help with new guests, and I followed Eli to his office.

"So, what do you think?"

"I love it. You answered so many of my questions. I just have to wonder why the others didn't work out."

He raised a brow but nodded. "It's a good question, and the reason is they had their own needs and desires. It wasn't the right fit. We need the right fit."

"I know. I can see it. You are all a well-oiled machine even as you're learning the ropes. I mean, it's insane to me that you guys have been only really open for a year like this, with an additional year of setup, and yet it feels like it's home."

I hadn't meant to say that last part, but when he smiled, I figured it might be a good thing.

"You're welcome to live on the property, by the way," he said.

I nodded, my heart racing. "Roy mentioned that."

Eli just smiled. "There's a cabin for you that's close by, and when I say it's a cabin, it's a small house, one bedroom, not a studio like some of them. But we reserved some of the cabins for family, and yours is mostly renovated."

I raised a brow. "Mostly?"

"There are a few things that East needs to finish, but it's not going to be a problem. I promise."

"If you say so." I smiled as I said it and he smiled right back.

"Most of us live on the property just because it's easier, but that does mean it becomes most of your life." He cleared his throat, awkwardness settling in for the both of us. "I don't know if it's a big enough space for you and your husband, but there are places to live that are nearby, of course. You do not have to live and breathe and work Wilder Retreats."

I let out a sigh, my hands tightening under their own volition. "I'm divorced. So it would just be me."

Eli winced. "I'm sorry. I just thought...well...I didn't think. I didn't even look down at your hand to see that you weren't even wearing a ring. It's just the last time I saw you, well, you know."

I rubbed my temple, the stress ebbing back inside my body even after a wonderful tour and interview. "It was awkward, and I said yes. It's a long story that I don't want to get into, but I said yes. But anyway, I love the look of the resort, and if things work out, it would just be me. And having a place on the premises would be helpful."

For my bank account, but I didn't say that.

Eli met my gaze for a minute as if studying my face, wanting answers, and I had to wonder what he saw.

He cleared his throat and was going to say something before Naomi walked in.

"Eli, I'm sorry for interrupting. But Dodge is here."

Eli's jaw tightened, and he stood up. "I'm sorry, Alexis. I have to take care of this."

"What's wrong?" I asked, standing with him, alarm running through me.

"It's a fucking long story. Sorry for cursing."

"I curse a lot, so don't worry. Plus, aren't you all military? Or former military? Cursing happens."

He snorted, and I was glad that I made him smile, at least. "True. We curse a lot here. It happens. However, Dodge is the owner of the Dodge Family Resorts."

My brows raised. "Oh. Right. I've met him."

His gaze went straight to mine. "You have?"

"Him and his sons Brayden and LJ. I did a wedding on their resort." I didn't have fond memories either. And not that I would call it a resort, but I didn't say that out loud.

"Well, now he's here, probably just to annoy the fuck out of me."

I studied his face, putting a few things together. "He's less than an hour from here. I bet you he doesn't like the competition. He always used to speak ill of the owners that were here before. I had forgotten that."

"He hasn't stopped. Now I have to go make sure he doesn't make a scene."

"Do you me to go with you? I've dealt with him before."

He gave me a look and nodded. "If that's what you want."

Naomi gave me a thumbs up as she went back to work, and I followed Eli into the atrium. Nobody else was there, and the flowers and other designs were gorgeous, but all my attention was focused on the older man in cowboy boots, crisp jeans, and a tucked in button-down shirt. He had his cowboy hat dangling off a finger, and he smiled over at us, his skin tan, slightly leathery as if he had been out in the sun for most of his life. But I knew he had capped teeth, manicured nails, and a two-hundred-dollar haircut.

That was Dodge, Franklin Dodge, from what I remembered.

"Wilder. There you are. Keeping your guests waiting?" His voice was rough with a slightly withered Texan accent that never sounded happy unless he was drunk.

Eli narrowed his eyes at Dodge. "We both know you're not a guest, Dodge. What can I do for you?"

"I'm here to make you an offer."

"You know I'm not taking the offer."

Offer? I didn't ask, but I wanted to.

"Your little place right here, it's nice. It's going to do its thing, but it's never going to be our place. You're never going to amount to the Dodges. The Wilders are just what they are, *wild*. You're going to have to get over yourselves and take my offer."

"If you're done speaking to air, you can leave now."

Dodge narrowed his eyes, looking as mean as a snake. "You were trash before, and you're trash now. So is this place. It always thought it was better than it was, and has only gotten worse since you bought it. Don't make me regret even letting you buy the place." My eyes widened as Dodge turned to me, and he glared. "I remember you. Why do I remember you?"

I smiled sweetly, looking as if I were the perfect woman with polite manners. "I'm sure I'm of no importance. Have a good day Mr. Dodge."

He looked between Eli and me, grumbled under his breath, and walked out, his boots clicking on the ground.

I blinked up at Eli and shook my head. "I see he hasn't changed in the past few years."

"That man wants to buy our place, but for a shit price. I don't even think he can afford it if he wants it."

I frowned, remembering the Dodge property. "The

Dodge place isn't like this. It's a spa, part dude ranch. There's no winery. It's nothing like Roy's either. And it's run down."

"Well, he still thinks he's better than us because he's true-bred Texan, and we're just military shit that has moved in."

I narrowed my gaze, my hands fisting. "He doesn't know anything."

"I like that." He let out a breath, ran his hands through his dark hair. "Well fuck. This has not been the greatest interview. However, your resume's great. Roy speaks highly of you, and if you don't mind the fact that we danced at a wedding two years ago, or the fact that Dodge is probably going to stir up trouble, do you want the job?" He let out a laugh, shaking his head. "Oh yes, I'm totally the CEO in this situation."

I raised my chin and gave him a wicked smile, one of determination and a little bit of anger. "Oh, I'll take the job. Because I want to prove that this place can be it. Screw Franklin Dodge. We are going to be the best out there. And frankly, I need the job."

I hadn't meant to say that last part, but when Eli laughed and held out his hand, I took his and shook.

And right then and there, I knew my life was about to get interesting.

Chapter Three

Eli

I had never tasted anything as sweet as the feast currently in front of me. I lay on my back, with her pussy right above my lips. I sucked, and I licked, spreading her before me as I ate and indulged. I groaned against her as the woman above me slid her hand down my shaft and then sucked on the head, hollowing her mouth as she continued to bob along me. My balls tightened, and I sucked in a breath, willing myself to last longer. I needed to last longer, and I needed to make her come. I sucked more, taking in my own indulgence as I flicked her clit, and she let out a shocked gasp. When I speared her with two fingers, she threw her head back, that luscious mane of honey-brown hair flowing down her back. She came around my fingers and on my face, and I continued to lick her and suck, needing her more and more.

"Eli," she whispered against my dick, and I turned, moving both of us so I could take her mouth.

"You belong to me," I growled.

"Always," she whispered, her hands still clamped around my dick. She squeezed, and my eyes crossed, but I didn't stop moving, my hand flowing down her stomach and between her legs. We sat there, tangled with one another as we played each other, needing one another. And when I lay her on her back and slid deep inside her wet heat, both of us groaned, needing more. Always needing more.

"More, more, Eli. I need you."

"Always, Alexis. I swear. Always." And then Alexis came around my cock, and I shouted, my body shaking.

The alarm woke me, my eyes wide as I heaved out a breath, wondering why the hell I had just dreamed of that. Of all people to be having sex dreams about, my new employee/wedding planner/near roommate was not supposed to be the person.

"Fuck," I mumbled and then sat up, running my hand through my hair. I looked down at my lap and nearly burst into flames. Because, of course, I had come in my sheets like a pubescent teenager rather than the adult that I was. I was nearing forty years old, and here I was, having a sex dream and jerking off in my sleep. "How the hell had I let that happen?" I asked myself, and I rolled out of bed naked, turned off my alarm, and went about cleaning up after myself. I quickly picked up my sheets, stuffed them in the washer, walking naked around the small penthouse apartment. We called it a penthouse, but it was just a near mirror image of the innkeeper's apartment across the way.

Naomi and I were on opposite ends of the main house and rarely saw each other outside of actual work. Which was good because I wasn't sure I needed her to hear exactly what had happened during my sleep.

I started the washer, grateful that each unit had its own in the apartments and cabins, and headed back to my bedroom. The place even had a guestroom, which made me feel as if I were a lot fancier than I was, but I didn't bother looking into it or dealing with it. Instead, I headed to the shower and turned the tap to cold. I hopped in, reminding myself that I had a lot of work to do today to prepare for Alexis starting work on Monday, as well as moving on to the resort grounds. We needed to prep her cabin, even though her place was more of a small house, and then I needed to meet with my brothers and go over the rest of the week's activities and our quarter projections.

Somehow, we had become businessmen, and while it was my idea, it still felt as if sometimes I had led them down the wrong path. Because everything we did now was a risk. I was endangering my family's future for an idea that so far might be working, but it might not always. So, yes, it worried me, but I told myself that we could make this work. We had somehow survived war, politics, and our own personal demons to make it here. We could survive this. At least, that's what I told myself.

I did my best to push all thoughts of Alexis out of my mind since she was completely off-limits. She had been off-limits before, at the wedding, even if I had felt that pull towards her. She had gotten engaged that night, and I hadn't looked back. Hadn't let myself. I hadn't asked Roy who she was, and when we had been looking for wedding planners, I had lied to myself and said that I didn't need to think about her. That I hadn't even thought about her being a possibility. So I hadn't asked Roy for her number. Or how to even contact her. Instead, we had gone through two decent but flaky wedding planners, and I had to hope Alexis, the one from my dreams, was the one that was perfect for us. And if that was the case, then she couldn't be the star of my sex dreams any longer.

Yet I had to continually tell my dick that.

I instead focused on what I needed to, and that was the meeting with my brothers this morning. We had our routine Wilder brothers board meetings, even though only one of us really liked wearing a suit, and the rest of us went casual. But we were a board, and we met. It counted.

I finished showering, telling myself that I didn't need to focus on what I couldn't have and focus on what I did. Soon as I got dressed, my phone buzzed, and I looked down to see a text from my sister.

Eliza: *Lexington is thinking of you. I hope you're having a good day. I will be sending different photos to each of our brothers so they get Lexington time too. Enjoy your meeting. Call me in if you'd like a female's perspective.*

I smiled at the attached image of Lexington, my nephew. He grinned that little baby smile up at me, and I couldn't help but sigh. I loved that kid. I had only met him once since the adoption had come through, and while I knew they were in the process of fostering another child, this one older, I still felt like I needed to go up to Fort Collins again and visit the new family.

Me: *Looking good kid. And maybe we'll just call you to say hi. We miss you, little sister.*

Eliza: *Miss you too, big brother. Go take over the*

world, and remember to live. You're allowed to have a life outside of work. I promise.

I shook my head, my lips twitching, knowing that she was right, but I wasn't about to get into that right then.

Instead, I headed towards the kitchen, where Sally, the sous chef, growled at the stove, and I tiptoed towards the coffeemaker. "I'd ask if you need help, but you know I can't cook."

She ran a hand over her face with a clean towel and sighed. "You're hiring a new chef, right? Because I can handle this, I can, but I can't do this many hours."

I nodded tightly. "We're going to hire her today."

"Her?" Sally asked, her brows high up into her chef's hat.

"I know who we need to hire. *You* know who we need to hire."

Sally cringed. "Does he know yet?"

"Nope. But she'll take the job, she wants it, and he'll just have to get over it."

Sally sighed, then gestured towards the coffeemaker. "Can you start a new pot? I could use some."

"No problem. I'll work on this, since coffee is something I can actually do, and I'll send one of the guys back to help you."

"We're fine today. But tomorrow? Tomorrow, we won't be."

"Tomorrow, hopefully, she'll be here."

I just had to hope that my brother wouldn't hate me.

I made my way past the atrium and library, where a couple of people were already drinking their morning cups of coffee, enjoying themselves. I nodded at the guests, who smiled back at me but didn't feel the need to talk. Naomi had already been around, it seemed, and people were happy. These were the guests who had decided to eat in the dining room or breakfast room for their breakfast rather than in their rooms. We had an entire staff to help out with all of this, and my job was to help run it all. To make sure that everybody was where they needed to be. Naomi's job was to make sure my job was actually done.

I crossed past my office and Everett's toward the boardroom. Each of us had our own offices: mine, Everett's, and Elliot's were here. Evan and Elijah had theirs at the winery, while East took over the attic office of the farmhouse. We had offered for him to have the office here, but he had liked the place over there and it was near all his equipment.

If East needed time on his own, then that's what he would do.

I made my way to the boardroom, on the opposite

end of the building, which happened to be the room underneath the innkeeper's rooms, and found I was the last one there. Everybody else was already sitting around, eating breakfast that one of the waiters must have brought in, and nodded at me as I walked in.

"Taking your sweet time?" Evan asked with a growl before he dug into his omelet.

I shrugged, took the lid off my plate, and smiled at the perfect omelet in front of me. "Looks amazing. How do we eat this well?"

"We don't usually, but it's going to be a long day, and Sally wanted us to be fed," Everett said with a shrug as he bit into his own omelet.

I took a bite, the cheese and mushrooms and tomatoes mouthwatering. Sally was a talented chef, but soon, we would have a new chef to help her out, and that meant issues were coming. But that blow would come at the end of the meeting.

Elijah cleared his throat. "Let's get started because we need to clean this room out for a meeting that guests have asked for."

I nodded at Elijah and knew that while we used this boardroom for our meetings because it was the biggest place for all of us to work and get things done, we also let guests use it for their own purposes, including any event planning or if people were using our retreat as an actual event for their companies.

"Let's get started then," I said and pulled out my tablet. I had a whole binder full of notes, and my tablet, as did the rest of us. We ate, and we went over the dream and the stress that was Wilder Resorts and Winery.

"We hired Alexis then?" Elliot asked, practically bouncing in his seat.

I nodded and ignored the feeling that went straight to my cock at her name. I needed to get better at that if I was going to be her boss. I wasn't an asshole, and I just had to remind myself of that.

"We did. She moves in tomorrow."

"So, she's taking the empty house then?" East asked, making notes. "I know you already told me that, but I wanted to double-check."

"She is. It's ready though, right?"

"It is. I'll double-check that the pipes are running and the AC is on. She'll have to just deal with what temperature it is until she sets it, but it'll be aired out for her."

"I'll send in the cleaning staff right before, and we'll make sure she has flowers and a welcoming plate of fruit and cheese," Elliot said, making notes.

I grinned, wondering how the hell the combat medic

at my side had become an event planner, and though I knew it was my fault, Elliot was damn good at it. And he was far happier doing this than he had been before. We had all taken a dramatic turn in our lives and were doing something completely different.

"She'll want her own office, much like the other wedding planners," Everett put in.

"She will. She can decide what she wants to do and make plans with us. But she's primarily going to be working with Elliot, right?" I asked, and Elliot shook his head.

"No, I think that was the problem before. As long as we have meetings to decide what's going with what and how they don't overlap, you need to be the one that hires her. Don't you think?"

Everett's grin widened as he stared at me, and I narrowed my eyes. "Stop it," I grumbled.

"Stop what?" Elijah asked as he leaned forward. "Is there something going on between you and the wedding planner? There better not be anything going on."

I closed my eyes in defeat. "There isn't. However, that's fine. I'll work with her directly. Which I should have been doing all along."

"If you say so," Evan growled.

"Speaking of 'if I say so,' let's talk about the next winery event."

Evan looked at Elijah, who shrugged. "We're on target. It's going like clockwork, honestly, because of Amos." He knocked on wood for luck, and they spoke of the vineyard manager who had come with the place, who was one of the most brilliant men I had ever met. He knew his grapes, knew his wines, and knew exactly how the winery should run. He just didn't want the title of director, or winemaker, or operations. He liked his vines, but he made sure that my brother knew what they needed to do for the actual winery itself.

"We're on target for the wines, but then again, that stuff was already in place. Yes, we're making our Wilder Wines as our uncle did, and we have to deal with the strategies, and our bottling, and our next crush. However, the main things that we're focusing on right now are the tours and wine clubs. We need people to come, look at the wine, bring it into their stores, into their homes, sell by the bottle, the case, or by an agreement. That's what we're working on right now."

"The barrels are ready to go. We're going to be tapping another one soon. We have a harvest and crush, all at once. But we're getting there," Evan added. "Amos is the one in charge, even if he says we're the ones in charge."

I leaned forward, my omelet finished. "I know it's a completely different concept than what any of us were prepared for, and it might have made more sense for us to go into a brewery like Roy, but the winery came with the resort. With the land."

"And even if Evan over there pretends that he doesn't agree, he knows wines. He knows his grapes. And he's learning even more from Amos. We've got this down," Elijah put in, and Evan growled at him.

I just shook my head and moved on to the next phase of business.

"Okay, glad we have a wedding planner because we have four weddings coming up, who came to us thinking they were going with one thing, and we have to make sure that they stay with us."

"I'll make sure," Elliot said.

"Good. The winery tour and the next big event that we have coming up is working. On track. And sales?" I asked.

Elijah leaned forward. "Our sales manager knows what she's doing, has always known what she's doing, and I'm working with her. We've got it."

"Okay then. Next step, we need a chef."

Evan went still as the others looked around at anyone but him. I cleared my throat. "We had a temperamental asshole before, and we know who we need to hire. She put in her résumé, she's the best for it, and we need her."

"You're fucking serious," Evan growled.

I looked at my brother, hated what I was going to do, but she was perfect for this, and frankly, Evan needed to actually grieve. Or at least get through what he had lost.

"Kendall is the best person for the job. And she has the experience, the skill, and we know her."

"No, you didn't know her, or maybe I didn't." Evan turned away, rubbed his thigh, and I held back a wince. Everyone else was silent, though I knew that they were on my side with this, as we had discussed it. I still hated being the big brother in this situation.

"I know you guys have things you need to work out."

"We don't. We worked it out before."

"If you did, maybe you wouldn't be so angry like this. But, come on, Evan, we need Kendall. You know she's good at this. I can't just not hire her knowing that she's the best for this retreat because she's your ex-wife."

Even as I said the words, I knew they were wrong. Elijah blinked at me, and I sighed. "I'm sorry. That was wrong. If you can't handle this, or, hell, if it turns out that the reason that you got divorced is that she's a horrible person and not trustworthy? Then we'll not hire her. But we don't know these things, Evan. You're not telling us. And it's hard to find someone perfect for the job right now. Sally needs help. And I don't know what else to do."

Evan met my gaze, and the war of emotions going over his face nearly killed me. "She's trustworthy. Maybe a little too trusting, but, fuck, she's the best at what she does. She'll be great for the business. And I'll just have to get over myself."

I felt about two feet tall just then. "You shouldn't have to, Evan. Hell. I'll find someone else."

My brother shook his head, his jaw tight. "You've been looking. It's why we had fuckwad as our other guy."

"True," I said, my lips twitching. "But this is a family-run operation. And I need to get my head out of my ass and actually care about my family and not about a job. That's sort of what Eliza told me in a text today."

Elliot laughed as he leaned forward. "Same to me. You'd think she would just do it in a group chat, but no, she has to be individual about her telling her big brothers not to be assholes."

That made us laugh, but I kept my gaze on Evan. "If it's too much, you tell me."

"No, it's good. We've been divorced for years now. It's not like we were married for long anyway. And hell, we all know that I'm not the same man that I was when I married her."

And with that, Evan pushed back his chair, got up

slowly, adjusted the prosthesis on his leg, and stormed out.

I looked at my brothers, and I didn't know what to say.

We'd nearly lost him. Nearly lost Evan, and there was nothing we could do to bring him back. It had been his job to rescue people. To save them. But we hadn't been able to save him.

Not from the enemy. Not from himself. And not from a marriage that had nearly broken him, even though we didn't know the details.

So I watched Evan go, and I took out my phone, ready to call in the woman that could change everything or break my brother. I had to hope that I was making the right decision. Something that I kept doing often.

And hating myself for it.

Chapter Four

Alexis

While I knew many of my belongings and furniture were in long-term storage, it honestly worried me a bit that I could fit most of my life into two suitcases, a carry-on bag with my laptop, and a tiny toiletry bag. If anything, I could probably stuff everything into just the two suitcases since I had room to spare. However, living on my friend's couch while I waited to move onto the Wilder Resort told me that I probably should've carried even less.

Amy smiled at me, though it didn't quite reach her

eyes. She was probably tired of me, as I was doing my best not to be weary of her. I was grateful, truly I was. She had let me sleep on her couch for an entire week when she didn't have to. It was just that my six-month rent on my apartment had ended, and my next apartment had fallen through thanks to a credit score that had shocked me.

That's what happens when you get divorced from a man who did his best to ruin both of our credits on his way out the door.

I had lost the apartment, and couldn't afford a hotel for an entire week while my finances were in limbo, and had been scrambling.

And Amy had stood up for me.

Only now I knew I had taken far too much of her time and had strained what little friendship that we had.

"I'm glad you're finding your way. I mean, you had enough time to get over Clint. Now you can move on, plan weddings, and do whatever you need to do."

I finished zipping up my bag at Amy's words and nodded, doing my best to keep a smile on my face. "I'm trying. It'll be a good job. The place is beautiful."

"I've heard good things about the Wilder Resort, though most of my family does things at the Dodge Ranch if we actually do things like that. You know? Loyalty and all that."

I held back a wince, wondering if that was a pointed dig at the fact that I was going to be apparently working at her friend's rival company, even though I hadn't even known she had known the Dodge family before today.

Or perhaps Amy just really wanted me out of the house so she could prepare for her husband getting home from a long deployment. Her husband had been gone for most of their marriage, and when he was there, he cheated on her, treated her like crap, and was rarely even in the house. However, this was going to be their fourth try, and they were going to make it work, according to her.

Between Amy's marriage and my own, it was a wonder that I even believed in love at all. I was the wedding planner who wanted nothing to do with anything that came after the vows. I was going to make any brides' and grooms' day the best possible, and then I wouldn't have to think about what came afterward.

Because I didn't believe in it.

"Anyway, with my guy coming home soon, it'll be good you're out of the house. It gives me time to clean up and get ready for him. If you know what I mean." Amy winked.

I just shook my head, smiling for real this time. "I hope you have a wonderful break when he gets home."

"We will. We always do." Amy just shrugged,

folding her arms over her chest. "It's after the break that things get a little iffy, but things are going to work out this time. I can just feel it."

"I hope so."

Amy narrowed her eyes. "Don't *hope*. It *is*. And don't you worry about it. You'll find the man of your dreams again soon. It wasn't Clint, but that's fine. Maybe you can snag a Wilder brother. I mean, I heard from down on the base that they're all single. Single, sexy as fuck, and maybe a little damaged, but the best ones are."

She rolled her eyes and patted her heart with the palm of her hand.

"I don't think I am anywhere near ready to start dating again or thinking about love beyond my job. The people I will work with on their weddings will love enough for me." That wasn't a lie either.

"That's what they always say. And hey, maybe if things work out well this time when hubby gets back, you can plan our renewal of our vows."

"If you have it at the Wilder Resort, I'll be there." I smiled but knew I'd said the wrong thing again.

Amy cringed. "No, we would have to be at Dodge. You know, family first and all that." My brows raised, she waved me off. "Don't worry about it. Now, let's get these suitcases into your car and push you out, I mean, *get* you out." She winked as she said it, but I had a feeling it all had to do with pushing and nothing else.

Amy was done with this arrangement, and frankly, so was I.

That made me a jerk. However, I needed a break too. Amy and I had never been close, but we had tried. And living together apparently reminded me that no, I didn't have the best girlfriends anymore. Clint had seen to that.

We stuffed my SUV full of my belongings, as it was already decently full of work things, I hugged Amy goodbye, and I made my way towards the Wilders.

This wasn't what I had expected my life to become. I'd had a plan, a business. Clint had come after me in the divorce and had taken everything from me because his lawyer was a shark. I had been naïve to think that his cheating, money problems, and emotional agony would've meant the judge would be on my side. I'd been beyond wrong. I had lost everything. Everything.

I had lost my home, my business, some of my reputation. The only reason that the Wilders had probably even hired me was that Roy had liked me, and the Wilders weren't local enough to know what Clint had done to me.

Clint had told others that I would cheat with the groom and get what I wanted by blowing anybody that I could. He had canceled cakes, flowers, bands, all in my name, so I'd had to scramble the day of, and the bride and groom had never forgiven me—more than once.

He had done all that and then had taken the business name out from under me. Now I had nothing. Just a few people who believed me, and a home I was going to get with a job, while I lived on the land with a bunch of men I didn't know, and strangers that came and went with their vacations.

It was hard to believe in love, and I wasn't sure I would ever again, even when I had to fake it to make it.

I pulled onto the ranch and took a right towards the business entrance, which took me closer to the winery than before. I could see the vines off in the distance as people walked through them, some on a tour I could see, others working. This was a working winery and resort. People worked their asses off, I knew, and most of them had been with the place before it had changed hands. They had stayed, and from what I could see, the Wilders treated them well enough that they wanted to stay. And for that, I was grateful. It told me that they were decent bosses. And from what I heard, they were. Now I just had to hope that I did my best to show that I deserved the job. I deserved to be here. And that I wasn't merely their last resort.

I followed Elliot's directions, since he had been the

one to send them to me, and pulled into a small home that was, yes, a cabin, but not a log cabin. Instead, it looked like a miniature replica of one of the villas, the same as many of the others. This wasn't a log cabin ranch, no, it was something unique on its own, and it was gorgeous. Small, yes, but I didn't need much. I had nothing to begin with.

I stepped out of the car and took a staggering step back as someone walked out of the place, a small smile on his face, and while I didn't recognize exactly him, I knew he had to be Eli's brother.

"Mr. Wilder," I began, wondering why he was here at all or if I was at the wrong cabin.

The man snorted. "There are too many of us to go by that. I'm Everett. I'm the CFO of the Wilder Resort and just wanted to double-check that East got every-thing ready for you."

"East." I went through my mental files to figure out which Wilder brother with the first name of E that was. "He's in charge of the maintenance?"

"Yes, he calls himself a handyman, but he does everything. So he cleaned this place up and got it ready for you. Everything looks to be good, and Naomi, our innkeeper, sent you over a couple of goodies too. However, let me help you get your car unpacked."

I met his gaze and swallowed hard. "You don't have to. I can do it all. Thank you, though."

Everett just gave me a calming smile. "Let me help. Eli would've been here since he's the one that you've met with, but he has an interview with our new cook. Chef, I should say."

"You're hiring a new chef?" I asked, intrigued. I would be working with this person often so that would be good to know.

Everett sighed. "It's a long story, well not too long. As with the wedding planner position, we needed someone to fill in as our chef who wouldn't back out when things got tough. Pretty sure we're hiring Kendall. You'll like her. At least we do."

I opened up the back of my SUV and frowned. "So you know her then?"

Everett winced. "Kendall is Evan's ex-wife."

That would be another brother. The one who worked at the winery. "Of all the places, of all the chefs, you're hiring your brother's ex-wife?" I asked dryly.

"I didn't say it was smart. It's just the way it is." Everett shrugged as he pulled out both suitcases from the back of the SUV. "She's a brilliant chef, a good person, and she had the sense to marry my brother. My brother didn't have the sense to keep her, but that's their story, not mine. Either way, we're all fine with it. She's going to fit in. She knows us and is good at what she does. You're going to be working with her often because she also is going to be doing the catering for any of the weddings."

"By herself?" I asked, blinking.

"No, she has a whole staff," Everett said with a laugh. "We're a bigger operation than most people take us for, so she'll have a staff. We just needed someone in charge of it all, and she's good at it."

"That's amazing." I knew some of the scopes of the place, but my part of the pie was only a sliver compared to the rest of the business.

"We're trying. We're a year in and in the black, if you must know," Everett said with a wink.

I grinned. I couldn't help myself with this particular Wilder brother. "That's very good to know."

"They were in the black when we bought the place, so we're just trying not to ruin what they've already made."

"And add your Wilder touch?" I asked with a laugh.

"Pretty much. The wedding side is the part that we've had the most trouble with. Your old predecessors under us and the person before that just kept reneging. Now you know you have meetings today, right?" he asked as we walked inside the place, and I couldn't answer.

All I could do was look at the adorable place that was my home—mine, not Clint's, no one else's. Yes, the Wilders owned it, but this was *mine*. I was going to work for it. The kitchen was gray and white, white cabinets on top, gray cabinets on the bottom. And it was completely furnished with grays, whites, and silvers, with a bright red hutch underneath the TV. Everything was feminine and yet almost farmhouse chic. It was pretty much exactly how I would've decorated it.

"This place is gorgeous."

Elijah grinned. "I'll be sure to tell East that," he said with a laugh. "And Eli. They helped fill in the place with everything to make sure you would have what you needed."

"Eli did that?" I asked, my voice going slightly high pitched.

Everett just met my gaze. "And East. But yeah, Eli picked out some of the additional things for you. Naomi helped in the end, but this was mostly Eli. I'll let you get settled a bit, but you do have a meeting later this afternoon."

"I know. It's on my planner."

"You like planners then?" A voice said from behind, and I turned to see another man that looked just like a Wilder walk in. He had a basket in his hands, full of fruit, crackers, and chocolates, and grinned. "Hi, I'm Elliot. We've talked on the phone."

I grinned at him. There was just something about these Wilder brothers. "We have. It's good to meet you in person."

"Can I just say I'm so glad you're here? I mean, I'm a good planner, I always have been, despite what my first job was."

"What was your first job?"

Elliot shrugged as he set down the basket. "I was a combat medic."

"And now you're the event planner for Wilder Resorts?" I asked, surprised at the jump.

"Yep. And Wilder Wines. I do both. That's why we needed someone to help with the big events that draw in the people. AKA, the weddings. I was a good combat medic, but I'm a better planner. Which I don't know what that says about me." Elliot waved it off. "Anyway, welcome. You'll meet all the brothers eventually, probably today, since we're all walking around the main building. I just wanted to come and welcome you. I see that Everett already has. Though I think you guys have met before, right?" Elliot asked.

I turned to Everett, my brows raised. "Have we?"

The other man shook his head. "No, but I've seen you from afar."

"That doesn't sound creepy at all," I teased.

Everett sighed. "I was at the wedding where you danced with Eli when we decided that we were going to buy this place."

I froze, blinking. "Oh. I should've guessed that there was more than just Eli there."

"Eli's pretty unforgettable," Elliot teased.

I just looked between the two brothers, swallowing hard. "I guess a few big decisions were made at that wedding, huh?"

"Two years ago, everything changed for us," Elliot whispered. "We got Wilder Resorts."

"And you got engaged," Everett added, then winced. "Sorry."

"No, it's fine. You were there when I got engaged. In public. I'd like to make it a rule that we will do our best not to have that happen at any Wilder wedding. What do you say?"

"I'm all for that," Elliot put in. "Public proposals are ridiculous."

"Thank you!" I stated with a smile, raising my hands in the air. "And one day, once we're friends, and I have a nice glass of wine, I'll tell you exactly why they're ridiculous."

"We do live on a winery. I'm sure we can find wine,"

Everett said softly. "We'll let you get settled in, but we do have a meeting at two. Sound good?"

"Sounds good to me. I just want to thank you. For everything." I met the two brothers' gazes, and they nodded, both shrugging in the same way that told me that they were far more than brothers. They were friends.

Everett nodded. "We'll see you soon, and if you have any questions, you have all of our numbers. I'm not sure that Evan or East will text back because, God forbid, they actually use their phones. But Elijah, us, and even Eli will."

"I'm never going to figure out which one is which, by the way. You're going to need name tags."

Everett smiled as Elliot threw his head back and laughed.

"You should tell that to our mother. We were numbered for most of our lives."

"She sounds like a wonderful woman."

Both of their gazes darkened, and I felt like I had said the wrong thing.

"Our parents were pretty amazing. We lost them a while ago, but they're always here for us. Even if it feels like it's been forever."

"I'm sorry."

"It's okay. We mention our parents often because

they had to deal with us. So you didn't say anything wrong. And with that, we're going to move past the awkwardness and get into work. We'll see you in a bit," Elliot said as he gave me a salute and walked out, Everett quietly shaking his head as he followed his presumably younger and far more energetic brother. They closed the door behind them, and I stood in my new place. I wondered exactly what I had gotten into.

By the time I unpacked a little and settled a bit, going through my emails and what I planned to talk about during the meeting if they asked me any questions, I was nervous but ready to go.

This was the new start.

I had come here for an interview. I had been the one to come to the Wilders so I would make this work. I would make our weddings here the best they could possibly be and make us successful, because Wilder Resort was known for their tours. They were known for some of their events and parties, but they weren't known for weddings. Yes, they had them there, and yes, the weddings were booked, but they weren't number one, and hadn't even been with the previous owners, in the San Antonio area. Well, they were going to change that. With my help, we would make this work.

I walked into the main building and smiled at Naomi as she waved at me and then pointed upstairs, and I nodded. We would be meeting in the boardroom, and I would finally see all the Wilder brothers in one place and hope I could get their names right.

People smiled and looked happy to be there, guests from the resort area and the cabins mingling with what had to be some of the winery tour patrons. There was staff everywhere, but only if you looked for them. It was as if they were only there if someone needed them and did their best to hide otherwise. It looks like it was a well-oiled machine, and I had to wonder if that had to do with the place before it had gotten into Wilder's hands or if it was a bunch of military men who knew how to give and take orders.

My lips twitched at that thought, and I made my way towards the boardroom area, past Eli's office, and wondered why Eli was the one name that kept coming back to me. He was my boss, technically. All of them were my bosses, and even though I had danced with him once, that was two years ago. Lives completely change in that time. *I* had changed since then. I didn't need to think about a dance with a man I didn't know.

I stepped into the doorway and blinked, holding back my laughter as I noticed that all six, big, strapping men with dark hair, light eyes, and chiseled jaws all happened to be wearing name tags.

Every single one of them had a name tag that didn't just say E. Wilder. No, they had put on hastily made name tags for me.

At least I had to hope it was for me.

My lips twitched again as Elliot raised both thumbs. "What do you think? Maybe if you see the name next to the face without a cheat sheet, you'll be able to get it."

"I hope she'll get it after today cause I'm not wearing the damn thing again," the man named East said as he growled from the corner.

I waved at him. "It's so nice to meet you, East."

He smiled and it reached his eyes, thankfully. "I'm glad the name tags worked for now. I'm usually the one elbows deep into something dirty. That's me."

"That's a lovely way to meet people," Everett whispered as he shook his head.

The man named Evan had his arms folded over his chest as he leaned against the wall but gave me a nod and then a chin lift. I counted that as a win.

Elijah wore a gray suit that brought out the color of his eyes as he smiled at me and held out a hand. "It's nice to meet you, Alexis. I can't wait to see what you do with the place."

"It's nice to meet you as well. I hear great things about the winery."

Elijah just smiled as he shook my hand. "We are good at what we do. Evan over there, even though he's growly and a bit of an asshole, he's the best."

"Stop cursing," Elliot scolded.

I shook my head. "There's no one here but us. You're welcome to curse."

That's when I recognized that yes, I was the only woman in a room full of six very large men, and I didn't feel intimidated or like I was in danger. They all gave me space, they didn't tower over me other than the fact that yes, they were big, but they weren't trying to take up space or put me down. I felt like I was their equal, even though they were my bosses. I had no idea how they were able to do that, and as a woman who had been in many a room with groups of men who didn't even realize that they were too much, I had to give them kudos for that.

"Anyway, hi, it's good to meet you. I think that that's everybody, right?" I asked, and Eli cleared his throat. I did my best not to stare at him. It was really *really* hard to do so. Because this was Eli. The man I had danced with had practically pressed myself against.

And I could still feel the heat of him.

And that was enough of that.

"We're glad that you're here. By the way, if it's ever too much with all of us in a room, you let us know. Our little sister Eliza gets on us if we're too much."

"That explains it then," I said, and continued at the look on their faces. "I was just thinking to myself that you guys aren't trying to be intimidating. Yes, you're all big, but I don't feel weird. If that makes any sense. Of course, now I feel weird just even saying it." My face felt as if it were on fire right then.

"Don't worry about it. We *are* weird. Now, let's take a seat," Eli said, and I took a seat at one side of the table as the brothers all fanned out, giving each of us space to work and not feel crowded. That was saying something considering how big each of them was.

"I don't have a lot of time. We have a meeting with the distributor soon," Evan grumbled as he looked at his phone.

Eli gave his brother a look, then stared right at me. It was hard to breathe. "No problem, I'll make this quick. Welcome to Wilder Resort and Winery. You're here to help with us with the weddings and to help Elliot since he's been juggling it all on his own."

"And thank God you're here." Elliot let out a breath.

"This is what's on your docket right now," Eli said as he pushed a stack of binders towards me. My eyes widened.

"All of that?" Did my voice squeak?

"We've got six weddings on the calendar right now, and even more that we want to do. Because we have the space. We just added two for later next year."

"Six. Okay then." I swallowed hard. "By myself. Don't you have a staff? I'm sorry, these are all things we should've talked about before, but I just jumped into it after meeting Dodge."

The other brothers all cursed under their breath as Eli nodded tightly. "You're right. We should've gone over it all. And your duties. You have in your budget to hire one assistant since the last assistant went with our old wedding planner, and frankly, Elliot can't do it all on his own. I'm helping Elliot as much as I can, but we all have things to do."

I nodded at Eli's words. "My old assistant with my old company had to quit because she was on maternity leave and wanted to spend time alone with her kid. However, she might be ready."

"Send over her information if she's interested, and we'll give it a look," Eli said.

Everett nodded. "If it all works out, you can hire her, and the two of you can do the main chunk of it. Eli will be around to help you, as will Elliot, while you're getting your feet under you."

I looked at Eli then, ignoring that odd knot in my

belly.

Eli cleared his throat, taking his gaze from me for a moment before looking right back. "We have a lot to do, and we don't want any of our brides and grooms to feel as if we're not paying attention to them or as if things are unorganized. They came to Wilder, not for a wedding planner but for the place, so that means they're still here, still working with us. And we need to make sure we do that right."

I nodded tightly as they continued to go over what was happening and what would be expected of me.

Halfway through, most of the brothers left, leaving me alone with Eli and Elliot. And then, when Elliot left, off to have a meeting with one of the corporate managers who was going to have a retreat at the place, I swallowed hard and did my best not to stare.

Eli was all business, and for that, I was grateful.

I could do this. I had done this. This was no more work than it had been before, and my pay would be better, and it'd be more consistent here. I just had to remind myself of that.

When my phone buzzed, Eli gestured for me to look at it and answer, but I quickly ignored it, my jaw tightening when I saw who was on the screen.

"I didn't mean to look, but was that Clint?" Eli whispered.

I smiled awkwardly, doing my best to raise my chin and look like I wasn't feeling off. "It was. He can go straight to voice mail or call my lawyer."

"Is he going to be a problem?" Eli asked, and I had to wonder who was asking: my boss or the growly man in front of me.

I shook my head. "He won't be. And I won't let it. But thank you."

"Okay then. Let's get back to work."

And as we went through the binders, I felt more at home, more in my element. I had a new job, and I had a purpose. That's all I needed to focus on.

Not my ex. And certainly not the man in front of me. Certainly not my boss.

Chapter Five

Eli

For the second time in as many weeks, I sat across my desk from a beautiful woman. One with piercing eyes, a long and lean neck, and the look of someone who wanted to be anywhere but here and yet also knew this was where she was meant to be.

Only this one didn't give me the same feelings that Alexis had when she'd sat in that chair. Instead, all I felt were stress, a little bit of fear, and not pity. No, never pity when it came to her. This was more about loss. Or disappointment. Or feeling as if I didn't understand what was going on.

"Kendall. Thank you."

"For what? For coming in and helping out? You know this is the perfect job for me, Eli. It always was. I've worked with three different inns and a brewery just like this. I have the wherewithal, the knowledge, and the experience."

I nodded, tapping my pen against the desk. "I know. You were always top of my list, Kendall."

She met my gaze, her chin lifted. "And yet you hired Tony before me. And Savannah."

I held back a wince. I did. "And you know why."

"Because I'm your brother's ex-wife. The same brother I have not seen for longer than ten minutes at a time in, what, eight years now?" There was a flash of something in her eyes, but I couldn't tell what it was before it was gone again. "I'm not some kid with stars in her eyes. I'm a woman who's worked her butt off. I have the experience for this. I was made for this job."

She let out a breath, and I let her continue to talk. I may not know Kendall well because I hadn't been part of that marriage, but I knew she was a good person. I didn't know what had broken up what seemed to be a healthy relationship. I didn't know why my brother left her or why she hadn't fought.

Evan was tight-lipped, and even though this hiring would be personal, it wasn't my place to ask her. This was a business decision. I was hiring her. It wasn't even a full interview because I was hiring her. Meaning I was going to have to figure out how to make this work. We were struggling with just Sandy behind the line. I wasn't going to force her to work any more hours than she could and stay away from her kids. I wasn't that much of an asshole. And, frankly, it was a two-person job, and Sandy was working too hard. We needed someone to replace Tony. And so here I was, hoping to hell this was going to work.

"You are perfect for the job, Kendall. Your resume was always on top."

"Clearly not." She held out a hand and then sighed. "Sorry. I get it. Hell, Eli. I'm even shocked that I'm here asking for the job itself. I like the restaurant that I'm at, but I'm never going to be the head chef there. I'm never going to have the ability to make my own decisions. The boss's son is the head chef, and Anderson is amazing. He has taught me so much, as has his father. And I'm not going to get in any better position there. But I also couldn't leave that place unless I found somewhere to fit me. And Wilder Resorts can. I still can't believe you guys ended up back in San Antonio. I mean, I didn't even know Evan was here until I saw the job opening last year."

It was odd to have Evan's name thrown in the middle of this since we both did our best not to mention him at all. She seemed to understand it as well because she blinked and swallowed hard. "Anyway, you're here. Your whole family. Other than Eliza." She let out a breath. "I always liked Eliza. I was sorry for her loss. I sent a card and a soft blanket. I always remembered she liked blankets. Ones that she could wrap around herself, even in the heat."

I nodded tightly, remembering that blanket, not knowing where it had come from. But Eliza had held onto it until everything had changed, and she had realized the true nature of her marriage. "That was nice of you. Eliza always liked you."

"I always did her. Maybe she'll come down and visit you boys, and I can see her again."

That made me smile since I wanted the same thing. "Maybe. Though she had to have been a kid when you and Evan got married."

Kendall rolled her eyes. "Just a little bit older than a kid, but yes. She was young. But she was sweet. Now here I am, not begging for a job, but needing one. I need a change, and this can be it. I put my name down for the job before the old man left."

I nodded. "I know. And you know why we didn't hire you before." Because this *was* personal, even if we didn't want it to be.

"Now, what's changed?"

I met Kendall's gaze, and because I didn't know her, I didn't know why the marriage had ended. I couldn't tell her everything, but I could be as honest as possible here. "Because my brother is a good man."

Her eyes tightened, but there was pain there, too, and I had to wonder what the fuck had happened between the two of them.

"He's a good man," Kendall repeated.

"And I didn't hire you because I didn't want to hurt him. Because this isn't a normal interview. Not when you have the Wilder name."

Kendall snorted. "It seemed too hard to change it."

I didn't know if she meant paperwork wise or something deeper, but I didn't ask. "I was surprised to see you still had it."

"I go by Kendall, not Chef Wilder or something when I'm behind the line."

"They're going to know, though. They're going to have questions. And it's going to be complicated. But hell, working with family is."

"I never would have thought you guys would be into

the hospitality business, dealing with an inn and people and weddings of all things."

That made me laugh. "I didn't think we'd be here either, but when I saw it work with Roy? It just clicked. There was a piece for each of us. Something that had nothing to do with planes or guns or losing a limb. Losing part of yourself."

"Is he okay?" she asked, then she held up her hand. "No. I'm not going to ask that. Pretend I didn't. But if you're saying this is not a real interview, are you here just to say goodbye or give me the job? I need to know."

I wanted her to ask about Evan, but it wasn't like my brother told me what he was feeling. It was like pulling teeth to get it out of him, but this wasn't what today was for. "You're it, Kendall. You always were. You should have been before everything, but you know why I had to say no. Why I had to try something else."

She smiled softly. "You love your brother. I've always been a little jealous of how the seven of you guys banded together, you against the world."

"We were never us against the world." I shook my head, wondering if that was true.

"From an outsider's perspective, it sure feels that way."

"It doesn't feel that way with Eliza's new husband. Hell, his family outnumbers ours."

Her eyes widened. "Really?"

I nodded, shaking my head. "It's a little ridiculous." I tapped her folder again. "Okay, I have another meeting, but we'll talk with Elijah, about what we want, but when can you start?"

"Tomorrow, if you'll have me."

I blinked, surprised. "Really?"

"Really. I've been unhappy where I'm at. I mean, I love it, but there's nowhere to go, and Anderson's new wife has the same position as me. They only keep me on out of loyalty, not because they need me. I can walk away right now without putting them in a bind, keeping my references, and I can start here. I can clean up that kitchen and make it the best."

"Clean it up? How bad is it?"

"Until I'm in it, I won't know, but there's going to be change. It's going to be amazing. I'm good at what I do. The best."

"I've always liked your confidence."

She gave me a look, opened her mouth, closed it, and then finally spoke. "I didn't have this confidence before. I'm not the same person I was, and I hope your family understands that. I appreciate the opportunity, and I'm going to make Wilder the best. I'm going to make us a force to be reckoned with. Because I'm a Wilder, too." She shrugged, her eyes filling with tears before she blinked them away as if they had never been there at all.

"I have the name. So I'm going to make us shine."

"Good. Because we need you."

"Now, that is something that I've waited years to hear." She stood up then, held out her hand, and I did the same. I clasped it right when the door opened.

"Eli, did that manager come to meet you? We got a problem with the Shiraz, and it's pissing me off, but we'll get it done." Evan blinked as he looked at his ex-wife, at me, standing there holding her hand, and the clouds that filled my brother's eyes made me want to break down. "I didn't know the interview was still going."

I let my arm fall. "It's just ending, so you're not interrupting anything."

Evan didn't say anything. Instead, he turned on his heel and made his way out the door, only he did it too fast and bent wrong, his prosthesis moving at an angle he didn't. He was on a new one, having just been adjusted the day before, and I knew he was in pain, but it's not like he ever talked to us about it.

Kendall reached out as if to help him and then let her arm fall, and I cleared my throat, hating this. Wondering if I was making another fucking mistake when it came to this place.

"Evan. Kendall starts tomorrow. I have to meet with

Alexis, but I'm going to hand her off to Everett. Since Everett will work with all the paperwork."

"Good." Evan let out a soft growl, and I didn't know if that was anger or just pain. His back was still to us and he was leaning heavily on the doorframe for a moment before he straightened. "Welcome, Kendall. I'll stay out of your way if you stay out of mine."

I winced as Kendall just shrugged, even though Evan couldn't see it. "Whatever you say. But I will be working with the winery. So we need to work together, Evan."

My brother turned slowly, limping slightly, and I hated it. I hated that I couldn't do anything other than watch because my brother would never allow me to help.

"Whatever you need. I will say, though, Elijah's the one that you're going to want to talk to. Him, and our wine club manager. They work for the tasting room. So in that reality, we don't need to work together."

Kendall's chin went up again. "Whatever you say."

"Yeah, because you believe what I have to say."

"Back at you."

I pinched the bridge of my nose and let out a sigh. "She's working here, Evan. You're working here, Kendall. We'll make it work, but Evan won't be your boss. Just me."

"Well, this will be fun."

"Amazingly thrillful," Evan growled.

I narrowed my eyes. "Just find a way to make it work. You said this was fine, Evan."

"I did. Because it is."

Evan looked at Kendall for so long that I was afraid he wanted to say something that would break us, but instead, he just shrugged. "You always were the best cook I ever met. Your food made me fall down on my knees in rapture. You're a fantastic chef, Kendall. This job's yours. You've earned it. I won't stand in your way. Even if I am that asshole."

And with that, he walked away, and Kendall stood there, watching, while I blinked, trying to come up with what to say. Only there was nothing to say just then.

Finally, Kendall spoke up. "Where's Elijah? I should go meet him."

"He's in the foyer working with Naomi. He'll know what to do."

"Thanks." She looked at me then, her eyes dry, her chin raised. "Thank you for this. I won't let you down."

"I know you won't, Kendall."

"I don't think you do. Because Evan didn't." She shook her head and then walked out, leaving me wondering what the hell I was doing.

There was a knock on the door, and I looked up to

see Alexis standing there. I felt like I was off-kilter, unable to think or do anything. Instead, I just blinked at her, and she waved slightly. "I'm sorry. I sort of heard the end of that, and I have no idea what's going on, but I have a couple of questions, and now I feel like I'm interrupting."

I waved her in and turned around for my bottle of water and my bottle of aspirin. "I need a drink, but I will settle for this."

Her lips formed a small smile. "You work at a winery."

"Frankly, right now, I could use liquor."

"I can't help you with that. Maybe later. I'll add it to my list of duties." I liked the fact that she was trying to break the tension, only I wasn't sure what I was supposed to do next.

"To keep the boss drunk?"

"Okay, maybe not that." She laughed slightly, and the awkwardness settled in, because I couldn't help but want to lean close to her.

There was just something about her.

Why was I so awkward around her? This was Alexis. We'd worked together for a week now. She was my wedding planner. No, she was the wedding planner for the company. And worked with my brothers more often than not. She only came to me with bigger questions that Naomi or the guys couldn't handle.

"Anyway, I just have a few questions. I promise that I won't take long."

"It's what I'm here for." I ran my hands through my hair, over my beard, wondering if I should shave. I almost thought to ask Alexis and then realized that I shouldn't care. I should not ask her.

What the hell was wrong with me?

"It's about the Luke and Tracy wedding."

"I have no idea who they are," I said with a laugh. "I'm sorry. That's more of an Elliot thing."

She winced and looked down at her tablet. "Oh. I'm sorry. This is going to make things weird now."

"If you tell me the month that they're in, I'm more likely to know. I'm sorry, I just can't do it all."

"Oh, I get it. Totally not a problem. The Luke and Tracy wedding is the Cinderella ball wedding in two months."

I nodded, it all coming back. "Okay. Yes, I know them. What do they want?"

"A horse-drawn carriage."

I blinked. "We don't have horses. I mean, it sounds like we should with where we are, but we don't have horses."

She gave me a patient look and I shut up. "I know

that. I have four different companies we can use, or I know someone else."

"What do you mean, someone else?"

She cleared her throat. "There is an up-and-coming company, in other words, an actual rancher who wants to have a side hustle."

"That doesn't sound sketchy at all."

She rolled her eyes. "I'm sorry I'm not saying this correctly. The farm next to this place, which does not want to be sold but wants to keep as a working farm, needs other avenues for revenue. They also don't want to become a pure dude ranch. However, they do train horses, and three of their cowboys were in the rodeo."

"Oh. I guess we are out in the country then."

"I know, right? We *know* cowboys. Who knew that we could find them in Texas?"

"You know there are people who walk around here with actual cowboy hats and cowboy boots. I thought that was just a legend."

"Only when you get into the rural areas, once you get to some areas, it's more ball caps and trucks."

"True. Though I'm more of just a Levi's guy, versus a Wrangler."

"Good to know," she said, and I had to wonder exactly what I was thinking just then. "Anyway, they work with some events by word of mouth, but I think we could make it a thing here where it can be part of the event itself."

"You're not talking about having a rodeo or something on the grounds?" The paperwork that came with that nearly gave me a headache.

She smiled brightly. "I'm not discounting it, but that's something more for Elliot."

"The legalities of that with insurance makes my brain hurt."

"Seriously, there are other things that we can do. However, horse-drawn carriages in Texas isn't an out-of-left-field thing. When I was up in Pennsylvania for a couple of weddings, and they wanted a horse-drawn carriage, it was a little more farm than a fairy princess. Either way, I think it can be really useful for us."

She went on to go through a few more things, and I nodded, taking notes. "You know, this could work."

"I know it can work. I wouldn't come to you with a stupid idea."

"There's no real stupid ideas." I paused. "Okay, fuck that. There are tons of stupid ideas. And I probably shouldn't say fuck. Fuck."

She laughed then, and I had to stop looking at her. What the fuck was wrong with me? I was her boss. Technically, all of us were her bosses, and she worked more with Elliot than she did with Everett and me. Still, though, I needed to stop this.

"You're welcome to curse. We've already had this conversation. And I do think the horse thing can work out. And I got a wholesale discount with a florist and former distributors."

My eyes widened. "Are you serious?"

"I do believe that your brother may fall on his knees in effigy towards me once I tell him how much money we're saving because we're going to use them solely."

"Do you mean Everett or someone else?" I asked with a laugh.

"I was thinking of Everett, but any one of your brothers may do the same once they hear about how much money we're saving."

"And how did you do that? I thought we had good relations with a lot of our distributors."

"You did. However, a lot of those connections were with the old owners. Who did a wonderful job, but things are changing in the business, and we're changing with them. At some point, all of your guys started working with different people over time because of just distribution and other issues, but I think this will be best for us. Everett has to sign off on all of it since he keeps telling me he's in charge, but I figured I'd come to you as well."

I had a feeling I knew why Everett said that, but I pushed that out of my mind for the time being. "That's great. Seriously thank you, Alexis."

"You're welcome. I have met with all six wedding couples so far, and I just have to say, this is blowing my mind. I cannot believe that you six Wilders were handling this on your own for as long as you did."

I rubbed my temples. "I don't even want to think about it. It's a little ridiculous."

"Well, you don't have to worry about it. I'm here."

"I'm glad."

She looked at me then, her cheeks blushing a little, and I opened my mouth to say something, but we were interrupted.

"There you are. I see I'm interrupting." As he walked in, Brayden Dodge slid that slick smile on his face that made me want to punch him. "Oh, is this someone new? I haven't met you before. Brayden Dodge."

Alexis met my gaze, raised a brow, then stood up, held out her hand. "Hello there, I'm Alexis Lane. I've met your father."

"Really? And he didn't share news of your beauty? Shame on him."

I nearly growled and rolled my eyes at the lame-ass line, but Alexis just gave the other man a tight smile. "I didn't know you had a meeting, Eli. I'll let you go."

"We didn't have a meeting. I'm not sure why Brayden is here."

"Oh, I just wanted to talk to you. About the event Elliot has lined up. Well, *had* lined up. You'll hear about it soon."

"Excuse me?" I asked, keeping my temper low.

"The retirement ceremony that you had, they decided to go with something a little more settled, rather than a bunch of military hicks. If you don't mind."

"Wow, you really did just go all out there with the smear campaign, didn't you?" Alexis asked.

"Excuse me?" he asked, his charm leaving quickly to be replaced with his true self.

"No, really, it's okay. You keep trying to use those put downs during your evil plan or whatever. Just do your own thing, Dodge."

Brayden's gaze narrowed. "My dad goes by Dodge. I'm Brayden."

"And yet you're following in his footsteps," I added, while Alexis grinned at me.

"I see you've hired the right person. Someone that's on your level. I just thought I would give you the professional courtesy to know that the account that you thought was going to you is going to me."

"Whatever you say."

I shrugged, as if it didn't annoy the fuck out of me that I didn't know what he was talking about.

"You're so far out of your depth, Wilder. You should have just gone back to listening to orders and doing whatever your general said."

"You have no idea what goes on in the military, do you?" Alexis asked. She looked so fierce and yet I saw the fraying on the edge. She was nervous but pushing through, and frankly, she shouldn't have to be doing this at all.

"And I see you just like to follow the trails of any man in uniform, sweet. Missing out." He winked and then headed out.

I just blinked, holding back my rage. I wanted to punch out the man, to scream or do something that was anything other than just standing there acting like an idiot. "I'm sorry."

"Don't be. He's the asshole. Oh my God, who the hell does he think he is just coming in and flaunting an account that he might've taken from you? And, by the way, I know what account he's talking about. It wasn't signed on the books with Elliot yet, and he was pretty sure that we weren't going to be able to do it anyway with the dates coinciding with another wedding. That man doesn't know what he's talking about." She looked pale for a moment, took a deep breath, and began to pace.

"And, apparently, I don't know what we're talking about if I can't remember the dates."

"Because it's not on the books yet," Alexis said with a shake of her head. "It literally happened yesterday. You don't have to know everything going on here, Eli."

"I do. That's my job."

"No, you trust your brothers to do their jobs so you can do yours. You don't have to know every single little thing going on every single day. That's too much for one person."

"You don't know what it means to be the big brother and the boss," I said with a laugh that was a little too hollow for my own ears.

"All I know is that you work way too many hours, Eli. And you're good at what you're doing. If I didn't know any better, I would assume that you guys have been doing this for years, rather than just learning as a family."

"We all had some experience before, not enough, but we're learning. And the staff around us are good at what they do. But, hell, you didn't need any of that from that man."

"No, but neither did you. And I'm glad you didn't have to deal with that alone. I've always got your back,

Eli." She paused and ran a hand through that mane of hers. "You're doing a good job, Eli. Never forget that."

"I'm trying," I whispered. I moved away from the desk, and towards the door once Brayden had shown up, and I let out a breath, telling myself that I needed to step away, to not to be so close to her. There was something wrong with me, and it had nothing to do with her.

At least that's what I told myself.

I stood so close to her I could smell the luscious, sweet scent of her.

And there was seriously something wrong with me.

I swallowed hard, and she looked at me then, her eyes going dark, and then she took a step back, clearing her throat. "I have to go." Then she practically ran from the room, leaving me alone with my damned thoughts.

Jesus Christ. I might not technically be her boss, but I was crossing a line.

And I had to do a hell of a better job than that. I already had enough going on in my life, and worrying about Alexis and my whatever the hell attraction I had for her? That was going to be one step too far.

Chapter Six

Alexis

I turned off my tablet, closed my notebook, and smiled.

I was doing this. What I had been born to do, and maybe in a different way than I had planned, but I was doing it.

"Everything's looking good. I just want to thank you again for bringing me on."

I looked up at my assistant Emily and grinned. "I don't think I could do this without you. This is a huge operation."

"It is. Plus, if I wasn't married, very happily, I might

add, I'd drown in the sea of Wilder brothers." She leaned back in her chair and fanned herself. "They are handsome, aren't they?"

I swallowed hard and did my best to ignore her, even though she had eagle eyes and probably would know exactly what I was thinking.

"They're handsome, but they're my bosses."

"Not all of them. And I'm pretty sure Everett and Elliot have both been evident in that you answer to Everett alone, even if Eli is the one who hired you." Emily's eyes narrowed. "It's as if they want to make sure that you know that a couple of them aren't off-limits."

She sighed dreamily, and I was the one who rolled my eyes this time.

"You sure do your best to try to see things that just aren't there."

"All I see is a very handsome man who might not technically be your boss because of the way that the brothers structured things, but you still work with him. And you danced with him."

I froze, looked at my friend and assistant. "Excuse me?"

"Don't say that. Do you think I wouldn't recognize the man that you danced with at Phoenix's wedding? The wedding that changed everything?"

I swallowed hard, memories of that day coming back

to me. Sadly though, it wasn't only Eli's face that came to mind. No, it was what happened after the dance.

"I don't want to talk about that."

"Yes, Clint is a horrible person, and I curse him every day." She fake spat into the air, over her shoulder, then looked directly at me as I tried not to let my lips twitch.

"But he's out of our lives forever. And I say ours because I had to go work at a photographer's store in the back of a department store while waiting for you to figure out what we were going to do next."

"Emily," I whispered.

"No, it's okay. It gave me time to have time off to have my beautiful baby. And I have a life with my wife, with our child. And then it's given a very amazing opportunity to work here with you. I understand all of this. It's still frustrating, though, because I feel like we missed out on so much."

"It's over, though. Clint is gone. My business may be gone, but I have an amazing job here." I gave her a nod, smiling slightly.

"With a hot hunky man."

I held back a sigh. "That technically isn't my boss, but I still work with him. And there are rules."

"Are there?"

I shook my head, needing to focus on anything else.

Honestly, I was surprised I could stand in the same room as the Wilders without breaking out into a sweat thanks to Clint; the fact I stood up for myself as much as I did didn't even seem real. "Go home to your wife and baby. I am going to finish up a few things and head to my little cabin."

Emily smiled softly. "I can't believe you live out here. It's gorgeous."

I shrugged, trying not to make a big deal of it. "It was cheaper than anything I had before."

"He took your savings, Alexis. He took your money, your checking accounts, your retirement fund. And demolished the business. How the hell was he able to do all of that?"

I shrugged, embarrassment settling over my skin. "By getting an excellent lawyer who decided that everything I had came from Clint."

Emily's eyes narrowed. "Even though that wasn't the case at all. Your business was thriving before he showed up."

"Not according to his lawyer. And the judge. Yes, I got screwed, no, my lawyer wasn't worth shit, but I'm not going to make that mistake again."

"You won't. I won't let it happen."

"That's why having a crush or whatever you think I have on someone that I work with is something that's

97

never going to happen. I already screwed over my life once. I'm not going to do it again."

My assistant shook her head. "Alexis, for someone that works with love and sees it every day, you don't need to be this skewed against it."

"Do I see love? Or do I see a party? A day that they vow to one another, but that doesn't make it binding. We all know that that legal piece of paper can be changed in an instant. They don't have to love each other to get married. They can think that they love each other, but they could be making a terrible mistake. And my job is to not worry about any of that, but to make sure that their single day is one to remember."

"I should put that on your business card" my friend said dryly.

That made me cringe and feel about an inch tall. "Let's not. I swear I'm not always this cynical. It's just been a long day."

"And you have tomorrow off."

"Ish. Since I work in the same place that I live, I'm not good about taking time off."

Emily clucked her tongue. "Do better. Make friends out here. Have fun."

"You're starting to sound like a teacher with a magical school bus," I teased.

"Hey, she was amazing. She taught us all so much, and I'm sure she could *get it.*"

I snorted, I couldn't help myself as Emily waved her goodbyes and left me sitting in my office, wondering what I was going to do for the night. I would probably pour myself a glass of wine, as I was trying out each of the Wilder wine's vintages, and then I would sit in my little cabin and read a book or plan for the next day. Even though technically I didn't have any meetings with any of the couples, there was always work to do. Always vendors to speak to and ideas to gain. So there wasn't anything as official as a day off.

Plus, Elliot liked to meet with me randomly to go over his plans, so they don't interfere with mine. We had an entire online scheduling system that looked like it was made for the gods, but we liked doing things face to face.

Apparently, working with six military men meant that everything was on time and early. Because being actually on time was considered late.

They were godsends.

"Knock knock," a woman with bright blonde hair styled to sleek perfection and beautiful blue eyes said as she stood in my doorway.

She looked like a supermodel, and I recognized her immediately as the tasting room and wine club manager,

Maddie. I hadn't had a chance to go over there often, other than for meetings with Elijah, so I hadn't had a chance to meet and get to know Maddie.

"Hi, there."

The other woman grinned at me. "Hello! It's been a couple of weeks now, and you came at the end of my vacation, so we haven't had a chance to officially meet. Hi, I'm Maddie."

I stood up, held out my hand. "Alexis."

"Well, since you've been hanging out with the boys mostly and jumped in headfirst into six weddings, I figured it's time to have some girl time. And get to know some of the women that work together here. Naomi has a date, so she was invited but can't come. And everyone else with families is headed out. However, I have wrangled Kendall."

"Oh, the new chef?"

"Oh yes. Kendall *Wilder*." Maddie's eyebrows wiggled. I snorted. "I'm sure there's a story there, but we'll let Kendall tell us when she's ready. Come on over with me to the winery."

I knew some of her story, but it wasn't my business.

"Oh, I have work."

"Oh, I'm sure you do. We always have work. But you live on this property. When is the last time you took a full evening off?"

I blinked. "What is an evening off you speak of? I'm a wedding planner." I waved my phone for emphasis as it pinged with an incoming text.

"And I am the director over at the winery. We don't get days off when we work with amazing wine and people. I get it. However, you're coming with me. Yes, to my work, but we're going to have some girl time."

"Oh."

"Don't oh me. Come on. I need girlfriends. Be my friend. Pretty please."

Maddie held her hands up in a begging position, and I laughed, shaking my head. "You know, tonight sounds great. I could use a glass of wine."

"A glass? Oh, honey. It's going to be more than a glass. Come on. Kendall's meeting us over there, and the three of us can drink wine, I'll give you a proper tour, and we can enjoy ourselves. Kendall said she's bringing cheese and crackers and some other appetizers that she made."

"And here I am, bringing just myself. I don't suppose anyone has a wedding they need planned?" I asked, only teasing, but Maddie just laughed, her whole head thrown back, and she looked gorgeous.

"Not in the slightest. But don't you worry. We'll have fun."

"So, you're not seeing anyone then?" I asked, genuinely curious about this effervescent woman.

"Nope. I mean, I do have a crush on someone, but since I work with him, it's a little iffy."

I blinked. "So, I guess I work with this mysterious stranger, too, then."

Her eyes danced. "Ding ding. It's fine, though. I'll get over my crush. I usually do."

"Are you going to tell me who it is?"

"Let's see, tall, dark, handsome, and really great with wine."

"Evan?" I asked, nearly tripping over my feet since I knew that Evan was Kendall's ex-husband.

Maddie's eyes widened, and she shook her head. "No, the other one. The one that looks sexy as sin in a suit."

I giggled. "Elijah then. Well, I like it."

"Yes, but there are issues. Since you know, technically, he could be considered my boss."

"Evan's your boss, not Elijah. They're very clear about who's in charge of who, as if they're worried about harassment suits or something." That made me roll my eyes even as I understood it.

"You say that as if you have your eye on a Wilder. Let me guess, is it the wedding dance man?"

I nearly tripped over my feet as we walked across

the pavers towards the winery. "How on earth did you know about that?"

"Emily mentioned it. I know, I know, we shouldn't be gossiping. But come on, that's great gossip."

"It was one dance, a wedding two years ago, and in the end, I had more important things to worry about other than a stranger."

"Like getting engaged to an asshole. Yes, Emily mentioned him to me. Not with too many details, because she doesn't gossip too much and want to tell me your entire life's story. However, I know more than you think. At least when it comes to feeling certain things."

I wasn't sure how I felt about that, but there was a kindred spirit feeling when it came to her right then, and I felt like maybe I should go with it. "And I know nothing about you."

"I'm an open book," Maddie said, and I narrowed my eyes.

"You know, people who say that they're open books generally aren't open books."

"You might have me there, but you'll never know until you ask. As for dating within work, I know that there are a few people who have, and a few married couples as well. And the boys are very careful about who is in charge of who, not for that purpose, but because they like chain of command. And they don't want to be the one that's in charge of each other. You have six brothers working together, so they're very careful about who can boss around who, at least on paper. They want this place to work, so they put in strict lines. That I happen to fall under a line of the man that I'm not crushing on just is kind of nice. I don't feel as bad for staring at Elijah's ass when he walks by in a suit." She mumbled that last part, and I snorted.

"It is a nice ass."

"Isn't it the best?"

"Are we talking about Elijah's ass again?" Kendall asked from the doorway, her hands full of covered platters, her dark hair piled on the top of her head. Her smoky gray eyes narrowed on us, even though I saw the laughter in them.

"Oh good, you got Alexis to join. I was truly afraid that she was going to stay in her office or with wedding couples for the rest of her tenure here, and we'd never actually get to meet her."

I winced. "I'm sorry, I didn't realize I was such a jerk hiding away in my office."

"You have to clean up the mess of other people, I get it," Kendall said as she shrugged.

"Let me help you with those," I said, as Maddie did the same, and we took some of the platters from Kendall and made our way into the winery.

The place was gorgeous, with stonework and polished wood. It fit the same ambiance as the villa and main buildings. It had its own flair, with wine barrels situated in strategic places.

Maddie bounced. "Come on. We'll have a tour, drink a few bottles of wine, and enjoy yourselves."

"You say that, and yet I feel like if I drink too much wine, someone's going to have to roll me home." I shook my head, smiling.

"Thankfully, you live on the property. I don't have that opportunity," Kendall said with a shrug. "Not that I would want to live on the same grounds as my ex-husband."

I met Maddie's gaze as curiosity filled both of us. "I'm sorry that things are awkward."

Kendall shook her head at Maddie's words. "They aren't awkward. At least not in that sense. I never see him. It's fine though, I live close by, and honestly, since my car didn't start today, my friend is coming to pick me up whenever I ask. And she's a night owl who likes to say up all night, so I can stay as late as I want."

"And I'm bunking on Naomi's couch tonight because somebody needs to water her plants in the morning since she's out for her date."

"Out?" I asked at the same time as Kendall.

"She's going on an overnight camping trip with this

guy she's seeing." Maddie waved us off. "I have no idea who he is or what they're doing, though I *know* what they're doing, just not where. However, she asked me to water her plants tonight, so I'm sleeping in the innkeeper's apartment, but not having to do any innkeeper's duties since her assistant is on duty."

"I guess this means we can get our drink on," Kendall said as she waved towards the bottles and bottles of wines.

"I'm a little worried since it's been so long since I've had more than a glass of wine. I'm going to be a lightweight."

Maddie clapped her hands together. "Don't worry. We'll make sure that you can keep up. *Eventually*. Well, let's get started." Maddie let out a sigh. "First, we are going to discuss our wines. Our most famous are our dry red wines, but we do have a few sweets, blends, and a rosé that is perfect."

Maddie went into her spiel, adding a little bit of flair that I hoped she didn't use with some customers since they went down romance novel paths and included some curse words, but I hadn't had this much fun in years. I had Emily, yes, but Emily had her own life and friends. It just occurred to me then that I really didn't have too many girlfriends. And that said more about me and my pulling away than it did about anyone else.

Things were going to have to change. And as I chowed down on stuffed mushroom caps, a cheese plate, and a spinach croissant roll thing—thanks to Kendall—I looked at these other two women and told myself I was going to try harder.

I needed to try harder.

Around three or four bottles in, I wasn't keeping track anymore. We sat in the closed tasting room, full, mildly drunk, and giggling.

"I need to go. I'm going to text my friend to come to take me."

"I'm going to roll myself onto Naomi's couch. Are you okay getting home, Alexis?" Maddie asked, giggling.

"Oh, I'm fine. I know the way."

"Well, if you make your way to one of the Wilder cabins instead of your own, have fun."

Kendall blinked. "Just, you know, not too much fun. Unless you want that much fun. And I need to stop drinking because now I'm getting a little angry about thinking of you rolling into a certain cabin when I shouldn't be. Because he's not mine. Really not mine. I hate him. I have to remember that."

That was the first time Kendall had mentioned Evan, and while I met Maddie's gaze, she shook her head tightly, looking far soberer than she had before. We were not going to press Kendall for details, at least not this first time. But there was pain there, I heard it. However, it wasn't my right to say anything. Not when the girls had been good about not asking too much about Clint. Again, at least not this first time.

"I'm fine. I can make my way on my own."

"Or I can walk you," a deep voice said from the doorway, and the three of us froze before we turned, comically wide-eyed and everything, towards Eli standing in the doorway.

"Oh. Hi. You're here." I hiccoughed, then slammed my hand over my mouth.

"I am. It seems that you've been enjoying some wine."

"Don't worry, boss, it's my wine. I'm not getting into the stores or anything," Maddie said, tilting a little bit in her heels.

"Honestly, I didn't even think about it. The guys and I do the same thing. Although you know that half of us are beer drinkers."

"Blasphemy," Maddie said, hopping on her feet. "And I need to go."

"Go where?" Elijah asked as he walked in behind Eli. Maddie nearly fell then, and I reached out to steady her, Kendall doing the same.

Maddie blinked quickly. "I just...I need to go. I'll clean this up. Promise."

"I'll help you get back to wherever you're going. I hope to hell you're not driving." Elijah reached out and gripped Maddie's arm, and she nearly fell into him, doing her best to pretend that she was sober.

"I'm not driving. I'm sleeping on Naomi's couch."

"Good."

"What about you?" Evan asked from behind Eli, and I hadn't realized the other man had shown up.

"Me?" Kendall asked. "I'm getting a ride. From a *friend*. Don't worry."

She emphasized the word friend, and Evan just raised his chin. "Well then, I'll walk you to the front area."

"I don't need your help, Evan."

"You're tilting in your heels. I'll help you."

"They're wedges, not heels."

"Semantics, and I've heard you call them heels before."

"Whatever." She stomped out, taking her platters with her, leaving me standing alone with Eli as Evan followed her out.

"Oh, this is awkward. Very very awkward. You're not supposed to see me drinking. I don't think anyone wanted us to be seen drinking," I whispered.

"Then maybe you shouldn't have done it in the employee tasting room?" Eli whispered.

Whispered because he was so close. How had he gotten so close?

I looked up at him then, at his lips. I couldn't help. There was something seriously wrong with me.

"I need to go back to my cabin. But I want to clean up first."

"You guys did most of the cleanup already. Don't worry about it. I'll clean up."

"No, you're the boss."

"I'm not your boss, Alexis," he whispered and then shut his mouth as if he hadn't meant to say that.

Well, good, I wasn't sure I wanted to hear it, but then I did something stupid. So colossally stupid. I went to my tiptoes, closed my eyes, and pressed my lips to his. It was just a bare moment, an instant, but I groaned into him. Eli put his hands on my hips to steady me or to hold me close. I didn't know. But when my lips parted, his tongue brushed against mine, and he groaned into me.

I was too drunk for this, too easy at making mistakes. Clint had been my mistake, and I wasn't going to make it again. Saying his name in my head, it echoed, and a cold rush of water fell over me.

"Oh. Oh no."

"I'm sorry," he whispered.

"Don't be. Seriously. It was a mistake. I fell on your lips. Because I'm drunk."

His face paled. "Too drunk for consent. Fuck."

I shook my head quickly and regretted it. "No, not too drunk for consent. I completely consented to that. That was my fault."

"Alexis."

"No. I should just go home."

"I'll walk her to her door," Everett whispered from behind us, and I jumped, wondering how long he had been there.

"Thanks," Eli said gruffly. "I'm going to clean up. Though the girls already did most of it. I'll just double-check. Close everything up."

"And I'll get our girl home."

My gaze shot between them as I swallowed hard. I followed Everett, doing my best not to think about what just happened. About the huge mistake I had just made.

Chapter Seven

Eli

My eyes began to cross as I stared at the paperwork in front of me. I should be able to do this. I had done this before, after all. It was only forms to sign, plans to go over. I had met with my staff earlier in the morning, going over events with Elliott, and then winery items with Maddie and Elijah. But right now, I had to go through the stacks and stacks of papers that everyone else had given me so I could check them off my list.

Again, I was somehow the boss, and it was so unlike

what my life had been before this. It felt like it was hard to keep up.

But it had been over two years now since we decided to buy this property and make it our own. Two years of our planning and finding ways to make this work. We weren't complete newbies at this any longer. We were past the year mark of full operations, had celebrated the anniversary. I was two years past retirement, and I was a full-fledged civilian now.

We didn't have bosses other than ourselves.

We still had to deal with some government issues and connections when it came to some insurance, especially with Evan's ongoing fight with the VA, but we were different than we had been before. Our lives were completely changed, and if I kept focusing on this and the work I had to do, the people relying on me, I wouldn't think about Alexis' lips on mine.

I couldn't believe she'd kissed me. Out of the blue, and yet not so much. Because we had been circling around each other since she had started working for the resort, and while I did my best not to think too hard about that, it was difficult not to. Because all I wanted to do was kiss her again.

And if it wasn't for the fact that she had been drinking and that Everett had walked her home instead of me, I wasn't sure what else would have happened. But she had been drinking, and my brother had been there to help me not make a mistake that could hurt her in the end.

"Okay, how long are you going to stand there and look at your paperwork and freak out?"

I blinked and I looked up as Everett walked into the room. My brother was rubbing his temple, but he gave me a look that told me not to ask questions. Everett had had a doctor's appointment that morning and was only just now coming back into work. And if he needed something, he would tell us.

At least, I hoped he would.

"What?" I asked, blinking my way out of whatever was going on in my mind.

"I was just wondering how long you're just going to sit there and pretend to work and not think about a certain wedding planner."

I scowled up at him and flipped him off. "I wasn't just thinking about her."

"But you were thinking about her a little bit."

I sighed. "Maybe. I don't know." A pause. "But you got her to her house okay?"

Everett studied my face. "Yes. I already told you this in the text last night."

And it had taken all that was in me not to text Alexis myself. There were lines I could not cross. At least, that's what I told myself. "And now I needed you to say it. I needed to hear it."

"You've got a problem, brother." Everett shook his head before leaning on the doorjamb.

"Of course, we have a problem. We own a fucking business. How did we get here?"

"It was your idea, and all of us were up for it. Including Eliza, who helped us out. Stop freaking the fuck out."

I looked behind Everett, gave a pointed look, and my brother closed the door behind him. "I kissed her, Everett."

"I know you did. I was there."

I ran a hand over my face and pushed back the chair so I could pace. "What the fuck is wrong with me?"

"She's a beautiful woman that you had a connection with since you first saw her at that wedding over two years ago now?"

"Was that a question or a statement?"

"Both. But, hell, Eli. You've always had that connection."

That was the problem. "And I hired her."

"Correction, *we* hired her. We went through all of her paperwork together. It was Elliot who was the one who agreed that she would be best. Not you."

"And then I saw her."

"Then you saw her, and you still agreed with us that we should hire her. As a company. As a family. We have a chain of command for a reason, Eli. You are not her boss."

"That's a technicality."

"A technicality that means that no matter what happens, you are not in charge of firing her or keeping her hired on. That is me and Elliott. You have nothing to do with it. What you did wasn't wrong."

"She was drunk."

"She was sober enough when we walked towards her house, and I made sure she was safe. However, she told me that she was the one who kissed you."

"You spoke to her?" I asked with a glare.

Everett's lips twitched. "Were we supposed to just walk in silence to her place?"

"Yes," I growled.

"Sure, whatever you say. However, we did speak. She said she was the one who kissed you. And you didn't let it go any further. Not because you're her boss—because you are not. But because you're not an asshole, you won't take advantage of someone who has been drinking. Not to mention the fact, big brother, you and I had been drinking beforehand as well. Do you not remember the two bottles of wine that we went through?"

"I still wasn't drinking as much as her."

"True. But you kissed, now act like adults and talk about it, or never do it again."

I didn't like either of those options, to be honest. "I hate when you're trying to be reasonable."

"It's what I do. I'm the one that will deal with her. Not that I have to *deal* with her because she knows what the fuck she's doing. As it is, I'm the one who signs off on all of her budget items. She has a full range with Elliot to do everything else that she needs. She doesn't need you, Eli."

I narrowed my eyes, and he threw his hands in the air.

"I meant as part of Wilder. Yes, the two of you go through things together, but you're not in charge of her. I don't know if she needs you beyond that, so why don't you fucking see?"

I pinched the bridge of my nose, knowing the line we were walking was beyond thin. "I don't know, Everett. What if I fuck things up?"

"And what if you don't? We all somehow, other than Evan, made it through this life of ours without getting married."

I blinked, the blood rushing from my face. "Whoa, whoa. That's a little too fast."

"Bear with me here as I get through this," Everett growled.

"Okay fine."

"Somehow, in a profession where most guys seem to get married young and start families, we didn't."

"Because most of the guys that get deployed want a touchstone of home. It's just what you do. You get married young. You have kids young. At least that's what happened in our parents' generation."

"And a lot of the guys now. They get married young, they weather tough times, and they stick it out, or they don't. They have families, they grow. None of us did that. I know Evan got married, but he and Kendall got divorced pretty goddamn quick and didn't talk about it."

"And now they have to work together."

"And now they have to work together, but hey, maybe they'll fucking talk about it and stop growling at one another. It would be great if Evan could heal."

I knew Elijah wasn't just talking about his marriage then, but we didn't need to say that. Evan had his own issues.

"Either way, none of us got married or even dated seriously."

"I don't know about that," I said, speaking of another brother.

"Fine, none of us made our own family. We're just

now finding each other again after spending how many years without one another? You were in the Air Force for twenty years, didn't get married, and was rarely back with one of us other than through video calling."

"I'm sorry," I whispered, guilt smashing into me.

"It's what the job needed. It's what we did. We're not those guys anymore."

"We're always going to be those guys. That's sort of what happens when you give your life over to the military."

"And now we're trying to figure out exactly who the hell we are in this civilian life. It's been two years, Eli. Two years of all of us getting out when we could and forming this company—forming this family. We're working on it. Maybe find something for yourself."

"I don't have time—" I began before Everett cut me off.

"You do. Because you don't have to handle the load by yourself, we have each other. That's what you wanted, right? For us to lean on each other. Now do it. Try to find something for yourself."

"And what about you?"

Everett shrugged. "It's not about me right now."

"Is that just you pushing things onto me then?" I asked, ever the big brother.

"No, what it is, is you being able to face something

in front of you that is new and exciting, and it could be something. I don't have that yet. But I'm sure as hell not going to run when it comes."

I raised a single brow. "Really? You going to promise that?"

"Hell no. I'm going to fuck it up. It's what I do. It's what we Wilders do. So maybe you should change something. Eliza did. When she found Beckett, she changed. She didn't fuck it up like a Wilder."

"Because Eliza's the best one of all of us."

"Fuck yeah, now, just try something. Don't have regrets. Because I swear to God, all we have are regrets, but this place? What we're building here? It's a foundation. Build something on top of it."

And with that declaration, Everett walked out, leaving me wondering why the hell he had shown up at all. Or maybe pushing me just a bit and forcing me to think was what he wanted in the first place.

I let Everett go and stood there, wondering if he was right. But then again, he had to be because I didn't want to be alone anymore. What a weird thing to think.

I let out of breath, grabbed my phone, and decided I needed air. Paperwork would always be there, and I was at least on target, not behind, but not too far ahead. I needed a minute to think. Things were running smoothly around me, the staff that I had hired working their asses off but doing a good job of it, and I paid them well. My brothers all had their roles, and as the Director of Operations for the resort, my job was to keep the company organized. To keep it healthy. And I was doing it. I had done it.

Maybe I should think about myself for once.

People were milling about, and I spoke to a few guests, ensuring they were happy. Naomi and the others had everything right on track, and sometimes I felt like I was superfluous. As in, I did all the work to get the place running, and now they didn't need me.

And wasn't that a metaphor for my family just then.

I ran a hand over my face and made my way outside past the stone pavers that made a rock garden, past the barn and open area for weddings and other events, and towards the trees. The winery was on the opposite end of me, and I just needed a moment to think. People were welcome to walk around here, as this is private land so there was no hunting, and while we did have wild animals, the coyotes didn't come out during the day. And it wasn't like we could drive off the coyotes completely. I shook my head, remembering the first time I had heard them howl before bed, and from that moment on, I kept a fan on so I could drown out their noise just a bit.

This was their land before it was mine, and I had to remember that.

I turned the corner and kept walking towards Evan's cabin, since he was the closest to the place, and nearly tripped when I saw her.

Alexis. She had her phone to her ear and a frown on her face as she paced along the path, talking a mile a minute and taking notes on her iPad.

When it looked like she was done with the call, she turned on her heel and practically tripped.

I moved forward, gripped her elbow. I knew it was the wrong thing to do because touching her skin was always a problem. It had been with that first dance when I hadn't even known her name.

"Eli," she whispered.

I swallowed hard, telling myself to calm down. And to let her go. Only neither one of those things happened.

"Hey, Alexis."

She smiled up at me, her gaze distracted. "Didn't think I'd see you out here."

I raised a brow. "Is that why you're out here pacing in the forest alone?"

She blushed, and it was so pretty that I had to tell myself to calm down again.

"No, I was just going for a longer walk, yes in heels,

and found myself over here. I was just dealing with the flower distributor."

"Everything going okay with that?"

She smiled softly. "Yes. Everything's fine. The bride for the next wedding found out she's pregnant and has been having an odd reaction to a certain flower that wasn't in the bouquet to begin with, but we wanted to double-check."

I nodded. "Tracy, right? I remember that. Elliot told me."

Alexis smiled. "I'm very happy for them. They're excited, even though it does change their plans a bit, but they can do this."

"Good for them, then."

"Exactly."

She met my gaze before she swallowed hard. "I wanted to apologize."

I shook my head. "Don't. You don't have to apologize."

"For kissing you? Yes, I do. It was inappropriate."

"It wasn't inappropriate if I wanted it too." I paused. "Unless you didn't want to kiss me to begin with."

She looked at me then. Her mouth parting before she shook her head. "I don't know what I want, Eli. And that's the problem. I hate to be wishy-washy, but here I am. I shouldn't have kissed you. Especially when we're on company grounds."

"We live and work here, Alexis. When are we not on company grounds?"

"That might be the problem then, don't you think?"

"Don't apologize. Just, whatever you do, whatever happens next, don't apologize."

"I'm just now figuring out what I want in life, Eli. Things are completely topsy-turvy, and I'm trying to figure it out. So, I'm focusing on everybody else, and I'm so grateful for this job, and I don't want to ruin it."

"You can be grateful for the job, but don't be grateful to me for it."

She frowned. "What?"

"I'm not the one that hired you. It was Elliot and Everett."

"But you're the one that I spoke to."

"Because I do the interviews, but I'm not the one that has the final say. Not with this."

"Because of your chain of command," she mumbled.

My lips twitched. "Let me guess, Kendall?"

"And Maddie. They learned your lingo."

"Well, you should too. I'm not your boss."

She swallowed hard, then licked her lips, and my dick hardened. Damn it. "Okay, then I won't apologize."

"Does that mean I can kiss you again?" I whispered,

not even realizing I was going to say the words until they were already out. And they were a problem.

Her eyes widened, but she didn't move away. "Again?"

"Again."

Then because she didn't say no, because she didn't look away, I leaned forward, cupped her face, and brushed my lips along hers. She didn't moan into me, didn't groan, but she didn't move away either. Instead, she parted her lips, and I gently pressed mine to hers, our tongues brushing before I moved away. "See? No drinking involved. No apologies needed." My voice came out rough, my words gravel.

"Eli."

"Don't," I said with a shake of my head. "Don't just let me off nicely. Just say you don't want me to kiss you again, that you don't want this. And I'll walk away. We'll never have to talk about it again."

"We work together."

"We do, but a lot of people date who they work with."

"And this is what you want? Dating? Or maybe just a couple of stolen kisses?"

"There's nothing stolen about what just happened," I corrected. "And yeah, I do want to date." Again, I didn't know I would say it till the words were already out, but they were true.

"I don't know. I'm not saying it's you," she said, her free hand outstretched. "I've literally just finalized my divorce even though we've been separated for nearly a year now."

"I get that. It's probably too soon. But there was a connection before. You know it." I let out a breath. "When I danced with you that day? There was a connection. Totally inappropriate timing, but a connection."

"Eli. You can't say things like that."

"But I did. And we're both adults. It's not going to affect work. Just dinner. That's all I'm asking."

She met my gaze and swallowed hard. "Can I think about it?"

I ignored the disappointment, ignored the feeling as if she had punched me.

"I'm not saying no. But I like to think things through. I hope you understand that. I'm a planner. It's literally in my job title. I need to think. Can you let me do that? Because I haven't allowed myself to think about anything like this for far too long. And there are ramifications, even if we tell ourselves there aren't."

"Okay. I can do that. Anything you want. I'm not going to pressure you."

"I know you won't, Eli. And that's the only reason I'm even saying maybe."

She met my gaze again and then she walked away, moving past me, and leaving me alone in the forest.

Had I once again taken on too much? I didn't know.

But I sure as hell needed her answer and my own.

Chapter Eight

Alexis

Clint: *We need to talk.*

I looked down at the text message, at the seven other text messages from him that said pretty much the same thing, and hit ignore.

I didn't block his number, even though I should, only because I wanted to know what he was doing when it came to me. He wasn't any part of my life anymore. I'd pushed him out. I had divorced him. And he had taken everything from me. Including, it seemed, some of my dignity.

But I wasn't going to let him take my day. So, while I didn't block him, I was going to ignore him.

I just really didn't want to know what he thought we needed to talk about.

"Hey, are you doing okay?" Elliot asked from the doorway as he walked in, binder and tablet in hand.

I smiled up at him, did my best to push away all thoughts of that text message. Clint didn't matter anymore. All that did was right now and my future. And that meant with the Wilders. Working for them.

And maybe dating one of them.

Not that I would think about that too hard right then because I needed to work with Eli's brothers. And not let Eli tangle in every single thought I had for the day.

"Sorry, just wool-gathering. Are we ready to go?" I asked, looking down at my notes for the day.

"I think so. You sure you're okay?"

I smiled up at him, at the youngest of the Wilder brothers, and nodded. They all looked so much alike, with their dark hair and light eyes, but there was enough difference in each of them that you could tell that while they might have grown up together, they had spent enough time apart to find their own personalities.

I knew that Elliot was young enough that he must've been just a little kid when Eli had first left the house and joined the military. I didn't know what that did to a person, to watch each one of your siblings leave, one by one, until you found yourself with your little sister in the end.

I wanted to meet this elusive Eliza Wilder, now Eliza Montgomery. But only because she was their family, not any other reason.

I couldn't let it be any other reason.

"Why are you looking at me like that?" Elliot asked, blinking.

I just shook my head. "Oh, I was just thinking about how all of you guys look the same and yet completely different. Other than the twins, of course."

He snorted. "Yes, Everett and East are identical, even though sometimes they do different haircuts."

"All y'all are letting your hair grow out a bit, and with the beards? It must be completely different than when you were active duty." And of course, the beards just made them look sexier than ever—not that I would ever say that.

He smiled then. "Completely. It's kind of nice choosing my own hairstyle, although being forced to pick out my clothes every morning is an ordeal."

I just shook my head. "It was like when I got out of high school and suddenly didn't have a school uniform anymore."

"You had a school uniform?" Everett asked as he walked into my office, then held up his hand. "Nope. Inappropriate. Plus, Eli will kill me."

I raised a brow. "Thank you for not continuing on that statement, and do I want to know why you think Eli would kill you for mentioning a school uniform?" I teased, even as my stomach tensed up.

"Don't act coy, but we also won't force you to spill any details."

"What do you mean? There are details?" Elliot asked, looking between us. "What did I miss? You and Eli?" Elliot's grin widened. "Oh, I like."

I swore I could feel the heat of my face raise the temperature of the room two degrees. "There's nothing to like, and we are working. We need to go over different weddings and events to make sure that we don't criss-cross our timelines. There is no need to go over anything having to do with your brother."

"But there is something having to do with my brother then," Elliot whispered, tapping his chin. "Interesting. Very, very interesting."

Everett smacked the back of Elliot's head, at least a little playfully, but Elliot winced. "Stop it. She asked you to stop."

"Okay, fine. Spoilsport."

My lips twitched. "I swear, sometimes you guys

remind me so much of my brother, it's too funny."

"I hope all of us don't remind you of your brother," Elliot mumbled, then ducked Everett's hand again. "Hey, we're working. No violence at the workplace."

"He has a point there," I teased Everett, who just rolled his eyes.

"Fine. I get it. No more beating up my baby brother. And I promise not to tease you any more about Eli. However, you do know what our chain of command says."

This time I did roll my eyes. "Yes. Maddie and I went over it. You're the boss, Boss."

"I do like the sound of that. Telling people what to do. It's different from the norm."

"I don't think that's at all any different," Elliot mumbled, then quickly moved out of the way even though Everett didn't punch out this time.

"Okay, let's go over these items on our checklist, then I have a meeting with Sabrina and Emily later."

"They're the pink and roses wedding, right?" Everett asked, then paused. "Why do I know that? How did I become this person that I know things like that, and they're just used in everyday conversation?"

I moved to him, patted his arm. "It's okay. You're allowed to know what kind of roses people are using in their weddings since it's on your property."

"I bet Evan doesn't know what kind of roses are part of this wedding," he grumbled as he walked away, shaking his head.

Elliot just laughed. "Well, I didn't know. And it's on the list. But that's your list, not mine."

"It's why we work so well together, and I bet you Evan does know. Or at least he knows what wine they're using for the wedding."

"Maddie would be more likely to know, but Evan might. Just to annoy Everett."

"I like that idea," I said with a laugh, then followed him out.

"A person that's most likely not to know is East. Just because he does his best not to know anything like that."

"East prides himself on being solely a handyman and nothing to do with frizzy events like what we do here."

"Is he happy here then?" I asked and then shook my head. "Sorry, that's none of my business."

Elliot just met my gaze and shrugged. "I think we all are as much as we can be. I don't think any of us imagined we'd be leaving the job that we had focused on for so long so quickly. Eli was ready to get out, he had gotten his twenty in, but the rest of us thought we would be career. And then, well, life happened." He paused. "Or rather, it didn't in some cases." He looked off into the distance then, and I reached out, squeezed his hand. He smiled down at me, squeezed back, and then let go, changing the subject to an event he was planning for a retirement ceremony. There was also a yoga at the winery event that they were working on with Maddie, and it was just an odd influx of people and things to do that had nothing to do with their pasts.

And I understood it. I wasn't the same person I had been when I had been planning weddings on my own. Now I had a whole team that each had their own purpose, and I felt like I was giving something to someone. No, I never wanted to get married again, and I regretted even saying yes on that fated day on the dance floor when Clint had asked me.

But these people believed in their happiness and their love. So I was going to give them the best damn day possible.

We made our way through the stone paver area, smiled at a few of the inn's guests, and went through our plans.

"It's going to be gorgeous. I have a meeting with the next couple tomorrow to make sure that we're on the right track, but your suggestion of doing the joint bachelor and bachelorette parties on the party bus or trolley, that is, the day before, is perfect."

"Good, because they're having their all-out party the

week before, so that way nobody's hungover, but this one will be joint, and we can show them a little bit of our home."

"Because it's touristy, and they're going to want to see the River Walk and all of that jazz."

I rolled my eyes because no matter who visited, they all wanted to see the River Walk, even though I had been there a thousand times, and it hadn't changed.

Elliot's lips twitched, we went over a few other things, and I did my best not to search out in the distance for Eli. I knew he was walking about today, helping Evan with a few things at the winery and then helping East do a few building things. It wasn't that I was genuinely keeping tabs on Eli, but I knew what he was doing today, and so I was going to do my best not to focus too hard about that.

Because I needed to tell him my answer. If I wanted to kiss him again, to see if we wanted something more than what we had.

It would be so dangerous, so risky. And yet I remembered that connection. I remembered that dance. And the guilt that had spread over me at feeling what I had within me for someone who hadn't been my boyfriend.

I hadn't even had a full grasp of the situation before he had walked away, doing his best to hide the disappointment in his gaze when Clint had shown up.

Damn it, Clint. He truly did ruin everything, didn't he?

But should I date Eli? Or would it be a mistake?

I knew it could be. And probably was. Because while he wasn't my boss, I would still work with him. We would still live on the same property.

There would be no escaping if things went to hell. And they just might, because that was the only experience I had these days.

But would I truly allow Clint and his decisions to dictate the rest of my life?

"What the fuck is he doing here?" Elliot grumbled under his breath, and I looked to see two men that I recognized and I sucked in a breath.

"They sure are here often."

"They come here for retreats, specifically at the winery, since some of their influencers and investors enjoy the place."

"Seriously? Their rivals?" I asked, astounded.

"I didn't say it made any sense, but it's what they do. And honestly, I think they just like to spy on us and to see what we're doing."

"And Eli lets this happen," I whispered. I let out a breath. "Sorry."

Elliot shook his head. "Eli lets it happen because if

he doesn't, then the father or the brothers are just going to start a thing when it comes to East and Evan."

"What do you mean?"

"Brayden has figured out that of all of us, East and Evan are the two most likely to get riled up."

"In other words, they're trying to start a scene, a fight, and label the Wilder brothers as the barbarians who don't deserve to have a place here."

"Pretty much. It's not working, though we can't just kick them off the property when they're actually paying customers."

"I think you should be able to kick them off the property if they pay or not. Screw them," I said, raising my chin, and Elliot just grinned. "I can see why Eli likes you."

I shook my head, ignoring him as Brayden and LJ walked up.

"There you are," Brayden said with a grin. "It's good to see you here. I didn't think you'd still be working here," Brayden teased, and I wanted to punch the man in the face.

The other son of the owner, LJ Dodge, looked at me then, hands behind his back, and I realized that I hadn't met him before. Oh, I knew of him, had seen him in the distance, but we had never met.

"Hi, I'm LJ. You must be Alexis. It's good to see you. Or at least meet you."

"It's nice to meet you too, LJ," I said softly, trying to gauge his measure. Because I didn't know this man, and he didn't have that smarmy vibe that Brayden had, nor the aggressive one that their father did. That just worried me a bit more because I didn't know this man, and I wasn't a very good judge of character, as was evidenced with Clint.

"We were just finishing up lunch over at your winery with a couple of investors."

"Didn't decide to have it at Dodge Resorts?" Elliot asked, and LJ shrugged.

"We did yesterday, but they wanted to come over here. It's really good food. I love your new chef." He smiled then, and it reached his eyes, and I just blinked, confused since I did not understand this man as much as I did the rest of his family. "Kendall Wilder, right? We tried to hire her before, but my dad preferred Stefan."

Elliot snorted. "Of course, he preferred Stefan. Stefan worked at a Michelin star restaurant." I heard the bitterness in his tone that had nothing to do with Kendall and everything to do with Dodge.

"And Kendall is the best, though," I said. "So we're lucky that your dad picked another person because then we got Kendall. We win in the end." I winked as I said it, and LJ just smiled.

"True. However, I think I still get to win a little bit when I get to come over here and eat."

"Odd that you guys come over here when your dad keeps saying that we're rivals," Everett said, and I was surprised at the straightforwardness of his sentence.

"I wouldn't say we're rivals," Brayden began, but LJ held up a hand.

"My dad has his opinions, but they aren't mine. We have different strengths, just like we do with Roy's. We should be able to work together."

Brayden glared, but LJ just shook his head. "You know this," he whispered, and I had to wonder what the undercurrents were with those brothers since the undercurrent with the Wilder brothers was just as confusing to me.

"And that's enough of our dirty laundry," LJ said with an awkward laugh. "We just wanted to say hi since I saw you in the distance, and to meet you finally, Alexis. I'm not going to try to poach you. However, if you ever find yourself wanting to add additional work to your load, give us a call."

"She's just fine where she is," Everett bit out.

"He's right. The Wilder Resort is doing well enough that I'm right at my peak. And happy with it." I grinned as I said it, and Brayden narrowed his eyes while LJ laughed.

"I get the point. And I'm not actually poaching. I promise."

"Sure sounds like it," Everett growled.

"Have a good day, you guys. We have a couple of meetings to get to," Elliot said as he nodded tightly and pulled us away. The Dodge brothers walked the opposite way towards their cars, and I just shook my head at them.

"What was that about?" I asked.

"I have no idea," Elliot answered with a sigh. "They confuse me. Which I think is the point sometimes."

"I cannot stand Dodge or Brayden, but it kind of worries me that I think I might like LJ."

"Don't let Eli hear you say that," Everett grumbled.

I narrowed my eyes. "And I can't get a bead on him either. For all I know, he's lulling us into a sense of security."

Everett scowled. "Or he's like Roy and trying to get us to work with him."

"Don't even put that into the universe," Elliot whispered. "Not when Dodge keeps trying to outbid us and cut into our margins."

I nearly tripped over my feet. "Really?"

"Really. It's like he wants to fight with every single

little event that we have. That's why we wanted you. So we had double the power," Elliot whispered and then grimaced as we noticed someone else walking towards us. "And I shouldn't air our dirty laundry."

"Did the brothers just leave?" Eli asked as he looked between the three of us.

"They did. Don't worry. I'm not leaving with them," I teased.

If anything, Eli's gaze stormed even more. "They tried to take you? Seriously?"

"First, not in the way that you're thinking, or the way that you just phrased it. I'm not going to go with another company. I'm with you guys. This is my home now."

"And on that note, we have meetings, good luck," Elliot said with a bounce on his toes and practically dragged Everett away, leaving me standing alone on the pathway with Eli, wondering how the hell I had gotten into this situation.

"They didn't bother you, though?" Eli asked, pulling me back to watch him. I wanted to reach out, cup his cheek, and tell him everything was going to be okay. And that should worry me.

Because I needed to ignore the connection.

Even if I knew I wouldn't.

"They didn't do anything. Just said hello, and they had lunch at the winery."

"I still think it's weird. It's not like we go eat over there."

"Maybe you should," I blurted, and he raised his brows. "I'm just saying, maybe they're not just trying to be bullies."

"They keep trying to steal every event that we have and constantly come over here to try to intimidate us."

"Okay, fine, don't go there for lunch. However, they're not important right now. We're doing great. The whole company is. Just remember that."

Eli met my gaze, and I knew he wanted to ask to see if I had an answer. But he wouldn't come out and say it because he wasn't going to push me. Because that's not who that man was.

So instead, I licked my lips, watched his gaze go to the action, and swallowed hard.

"Okay," I whispered, and he blinked.

"Okay?"

"Okay. Let's go on a date. Let's try it out."

"Why?" he blurted, then laughed. "I mean, why did you suddenly have an answer. Not why that you're going out with me. Because I'm not going to ask that, I don't really want to know the answer."

That made me laugh, and I shook my head.

"Because I'm tired of comparing everybody to Clint. That's what I keep doing. My divorce is final. I'm single, and I want to."

And that's all I'm going to say.

"Good. I have to promise that we're not going to screw this up."

The intensity in his gaze scared me, and I swallowed hard again. "We're not going to fuck this up."

And I had to hope that neither one of us was lying to each other.

Chapter Nine

Eli

This was probably a mistake, but I was getting pretty good at making them.

I walked across the path to Alexis' home and told myself that this wasn't a huge mistake. However, the fact that I could *walk* to her place rather than drive, meant that things were probably far more complicated than they needed to be.

I hadn't known if she would take the offer to live on the property or not until she had said yes. I had known that she was between jobs because of circumstances outside of her control, but I hadn't realized that she had needed a place to live. Maybe we would talk about that tonight. Or maybe that would be too tough. Hell, just because I couldn't get the woman out of my mind even when I should, didn't mean I needed to know each of her deep dark secrets.

But I wanted to know them.

I didn't have those deep dark secrets, not like my brothers did. At least, I didn't think I did. So, perhaps she wouldn't run away.

"Hell," I mumbled under my breath, but I knocked on her door and rolled my shoulders back.

She opened it quickly as if she had been waiting there, or maybe I had blanked out, seeing too much into everything once again.

She stood there in a black dress that hugged her curves, high heels that did horrible things to my imagination, and had let her hair fall loosely around her face. It was in long waves, and she looked absolutely gorgeous.

There was seriously something wrong with me because all I wanted to do was push her inside that house of hers, ruck up that dress, and see exactly what she wore underneath.

And from the way that her eyes met mine, the heat in that gaze of hers, I hoped she was thinking the same thing. But, this was a first date. We should probably actually have the first date first.

"You're right on time. And when you said you would meet me to pick me up here, I didn't think about the fact that we'd have to double back to your car."

"It's okay. I honestly thought about driving back here to pick you up, but then we wouldn't be able to walk past some of the pathways, which are the best parts of the area."

"You're right. This is a gorgeous piece of land, and I still can't believe I get to live here."

"I don't believe it either. Not that you live here, but that I do." I shook my head, pinched the bridge of my nose. "I swear I'm better at words than it sounds."

She laughed, closed and locked the door behind her. "I swear I'm better at them too. Sometimes. Okay, so we're going to Chama Gaucha?"

"You look nice," I said after a moment, clearing my throat.

"I was thinking the same thing. I know we're going to the Brazilian steakhouse, and I wasn't sure what to wear. I actually looked online to see what people were wearing on Instagram."

I snorted as I led her down the moonlit path towards my car. "You know, I almost said the same thing. It probably would've been a better idea than me having to ask Kendall."

Alexis tripped on her heels, and I cupped her elbow.

"Asking Kendall would've been so smart. So, you had no idea either?"

"I've been to Brazilian steakhouses before, but they're a little more casual than this one. Kendall told me to wear nice pants, but no tie or jacket needed. Which is good because I hate wearing a damn tie."

"I don't know. I think you would look nice in a suit. Just saying." Her gaze raked my body, and my cock went hard.

Damn it, just one look, and I was ready to bend her over to the front of my truck.

There was something seriously wrong with me.

I helped her into the truck, and we made our way down the road and hopped onto the highway, heading towards the Brazilian place. It was an easy twenty-five minutes away from Wilders, but in Texas, that was like a minute drive to get milk.

It was something that took getting used to, considering at one point I used to live in a huge suburban city and didn't even have a car since I didn't need one on base.

We spoke of work and nothing too personal, as it was our common ground for now. And when Roy's name came up, her eyes brightened, and she laughed, and I would've felt jealous if I didn't see the deep respect in her eyes and hear it in her tone, I knew it was

147

nothing more than what I felt for the man. Just a good sense of *right*.

She smiled. "I owe him so much."

I frowned as I helped her out of the truck and we headed towards the entryway. The damn place even had a valet, though I parked my beast myself. I needed it on the resort, although I kind of wish I had a sleek car for the night. I probably should have borrowed one for the date, but this was me, and Alexis needed to get to know the real me. Which was an odd sentence to think at all, considering I had spent my life being good about just being casual.

"Why do you say that?" I asked, bringing myself back to the conversation.

"That will take a drink to explain." She winced when she said it, but I nodded, understanding.

"Okay. Well, I hear they have an amazing bar."

"Good, because I'm nervous." She cringed. "Since this is my first date since my divorce. Which is kind of sad if you think about it."

I shook my head and gripped her hand. She looked at me then, and we both paused, the connection hitting again, that feeling as if I had known her for longer than this.

"It's okay. I kind of like being your first." I winked as

I said it, and she rolled her eyes, that smile coming back, one I had wanted desperately to see.

I gave the hostess my name, and she looked up our reservation before she headed us back to our table.

"This place is swanky," Alexis whispered underneath her breath as I grinned.

"Yeah, this is where Everett told me to come. I've always wanted to because, hello, meat. But I'm really glad that we had a good quarter, because hell, this probably is going to cost an arm and a leg. Or my firstborn."

"We can go somewhere else," Alexis said quickly as she sat down, and a waiter took her purse and set it on its own chair with a little purse hook. My mind boggled, and Alexis just smiled and thanked the host before sitting properly.

"We're fine, I'm taking you out to a nice place, and Everett wouldn't steer us wrong, but does your purse have its own pillow? Its own chair?"

"Yes. Some of them do that. This one's more of a hook. I've been to one place, when I was in Paris, it actually had its own throne."

"I really feel like I don't fit in here."

"You were an officer in the military, bet you fit in more than your brothers feel sometimes. Other than Everett."

"You know what's funny? Elijah's the one that's

better off in a suit. Everett plays well, but it's Elijah who can really pull it off."

"Then you just fake it till you make it. I know this because of the different distributors and venues that I work with. Or I worked with. It's a little bit different having just the one menu to work with and people coming to you."

"So, is this where we start to talk about it?" I asked as the waitress came over to ask about drinks. I ordered an old fashioned because it sounded fancy and I actually liked it, while Alexis ordered a vodka martini.

It was easy to order here, because you got the salad and meat, and just enjoyed yourselves. People would walk around you with meat on swords, and then if you had your green card up, they would slice you some meat. If it was flipped to red, then they wouldn't come to you. I was just excited because hello, all-you-can-eat meat? The best thing.

"How's your old fashioned?" Alexis asked after a minute, and I took a sip, the smoky flavor just right.

"Good. I'm kind of glad that these came back into fashion. With all those little whiskey distilleries and bars popping up all over the cities."

"I know the young are finding it new again, so we can drink it."

"Excuse me. We *are* the young."

"We are in our thirties, Eli. We are officially part of the older generation."

I shuddered but then nodded. "I'm okay with that. I was a dumbass when I was in my twenties, so I'm okay with being the old man at nearly thirty-eight."

"And I'm okay with being the matronly divorcée at thirty."

"There's nothing matronly about you, Alexis."

"Well, that was a better line than before."

I rolled my eyes, took another sip of my drink.

"Want to go get our salads and sides before we start divulging in the meat?" I paused. "See, now I don't think I could ever come here with just my brothers."

"What? All the dick jokes are going to be a little bit too much for you?" she asked. The butter-wouldn't-melt-in-her-mouth smile was just too much.

I leaned forward over the table, kissed her softly, watched that surprise flicker her over her face once more, and then stood up. "Let's go get you some salad and green beans or whatever the hell else they give us, and then we are going to eat some meat. And enjoy it."

"Whatever you say, Mr. Wilder."

"I like the sound of that," I mumbled, and she pushed at my arm playfully as we walked over to get our sides.

I had been to a Brazilian steakhouse before, but this

was about five times the amount of food, and the service was five-star. I literally couldn't believe all of this would be included, and I was very glad that I had a healthy appetite. From the way that Alexis piled up sides on her plate, she was going for it as well. I was slowly falling in love with the woman, and it was all because of the food. There was something seriously wrong with me.

We sat back down, began to eat, and when the men with swords of meat came by, we each took a sliver of filet, lamb, chicken, rib eye, countless others. The bacon-wrapped filet nearly made me orgasm right at the table, as did Alexis, as we both moaned, and we kept going until finally, we slid the cards to red so we could take a break and just enjoy ourselves.

"They were so fast," she whispered.

"I'm sure there's a joke there about being fast with their meat, but I can't talk, I have meat in my mouth, and that's all I want. Oh my God, this is so good." I groaned as I said it, and she laughed, shaking her head.

"I'm so glad that we can joke about this."

"What? There's got to be dick jokes when you are talking about this place."

We whispered as we said it, as we didn't really want anyone else to hear us saying these things in a swanky place, but it's what happens.

"Okay, you're on your second drink. Talk to me."

She sighed but shrugged, sipping her martini. "Well, I said yes to Clint at that wedding."

I frowned, doing my best not to grind my teeth.

"I see that look on your face, and I felt it too, that connection. And I shouldn't have because I was dating someone then. But I did."

I opened my mouth to say something, but she held up her hand.

"Let me just get this all out."

"I'm here."

And I wanted to know.

"I said yes because I wanted to. But I didn't expect the proposal like that, or even right then. I thought we had more time to figure out exactly what each other wanted, but I was wrong. Clint wanted the big splashy affair, and I was a wedding planner, so I made sure it happened. And Emily helped. She's amazing."

I nodded, thinking of her assistant.

"I had a business. I was my own CEO, CFO, everything. Emily did a lot, but she is a married woman and a mother now and has her own life. The way that we were working before worked perfectly. So Emily could have her life, and I could work myself to the bone without even thinking about it."

"I don't know if that's the healthy way to think about it," I mumbled.

"You're right. And things would've had to change, but I was already thinking about hiring an assistant for Emily, or at least a cohort. We were trying to think of a title so Emily wouldn't feel shuffled to the side, you know?"

"I get it. Though I guess with you working with Elliot the way that you are, with Elliot's team, you don't need that here?"

She shook ahead.

"No, and if I did, I would first figure out how to rearrange things to save money, and then I would come to you. I'm not going to work myself like that again. I promise."

"Good, but it's my job to make sure you don't in the first place."

"I guess so." Her smile fell then, and she sighed. "Anyway, I was working too hard, and I knew it. But Clint did too. And Clint likes nice things, so he works for it."

I heard the edge of her tone as she said that, and I frowned. "There was trouble there then?"

"I didn't realize it at first. He liked to spend money, and he liked the finer things. And I didn't have that kind of money. Not the way he thought I did. And because of that, he was resentful. He wanted me to be the wife I wasn't."

"Why would he think that you would have money?" I asked, honestly confused. That didn't really make sense.

She sighed, drank another big gulp of her martini, and played with the food on her plate. "I come from money."

I blinked. "What? Really?"

"I try not to tell people, but my grandparents on my mother's side had a lot of money. We're talking a lot," she whispered and then shrugged. "That's why I know about the purse thing, and while I can be the perfect chameleon at certain weddings or even a place like this. And I've been to Michelin star restaurants where even to get a table it's a thousand dollars a plate."

"Jesus Christ," I grumbled and took another sip of my beer. I'd switched to beer after the old fashioned, but I only was going to have the two drinks and tons of water to go with all the meat so I could drive home.

"Yeah. My grandparents were loaded but didn't give us any money. Which makes sense because we each had our own businesses, and everything worked out well."

"But Clint thought you had more?"

"He knew my grandparents and thought I had a direct line to that money. I didn't. All I had was a trust."

"A trust," I said, feeling like I was three steps behind.

She ran her hand through her hair, then winced before fluffing it back into place. "My grandfather died three years ago, and my grandmother was the matriarch of our family. I have amazing parents, the most perfect brother and sister-in-law, and a niece and nephew that all live in Spain. Even my parents. They all moved there to be close to the babies and my sister-in-law's family."

"And you're here. I'm sorry."

"It's okay. I try to see them as often as I can, and I know you understand what it means to live apart from your family because of your job or just the way that circumstances are."

"I do. It's why that we built Wilder Resort and Winery, so we could be together, even if it's a fantastical way to do it."

"It sure is that. However, Clint thought he could get to the family money. At least that's how it seems on the outside. I don't know if that was his true motivation or whatever. In the end, he got mean. He got rude. He wasn't a good person. And he didn't love me the way that I thought he did. In the end, I didn't love him either."

"Alexis, I'm sorry."

"So am I. The thing is, I lost my grandmother a few months ago," she whispered, and I leaned forward and gripped her hand.

"Alexis. I'm so sorry, I didn't know."

"It's okay. A lot of people don't know. Grandmother died in her sleep, peacefully, with no pain, the doctors tell me. She's with Grandpa now, and I know she's happy where she is. At least that's what I have to tell myself. Because I hate thinking that it could be anything else."

"So, I'm going to ask a weird question; what does that mean for your family?"

"And there it is," she said with a sigh. "That's exactly what Clint thought, but not the same way you are. My marriage to Clint ended before my grandmother passed. Because I couldn't handle it anymore, and Clint wasn't getting what he wanted."

"Sucks for him, doesn't it," I said slyly, and she snorted, finishing her martini before sipping her water.

"Well, sucks for him indeed because I do have that family money coming in, but not until next year because it has to be a year after my grandmother's death. That's the way the trust is written, to ensure there aren't conniving loopholes and other things. I totally understand it, and there were only some low points in the past year, the past few months, I had really wanted that money."

"Because of the business?" I asked, still confused about that.

"Clint hired a shark of an attorney, and that shark took me for everything that I was worth. Somehow they convinced the judge that I was the sole earner, and without him, the wedding business wouldn't have taken off."

"Bullshit," I said loudly enough that a couple of patrons glared at me. I ignored them.

"You're right. He had nothing to do with it, but the judge didn't agree. I had to give him half of my controlling earnings or sell. Sell completely and let it dissolve, lose my name, and everything. And so that's what I did. Because there was no way I could actually survive with half of my earnings. It didn't make any sense, and he knew that. He wanted the money. So he got what little he could from the business, and along the way, he burned bridges with certain contacts—at least that's what I'm thinking—so I couldn't land on my feet. And Roy had already hired somebody full time, and he didn't need me." She sighed again and shook her head.

"Alexis. I want to find this guy and hit him. Just punch him quickly. He won't feel a thing. I'm lying. He's going to feel everything, and I'm going to enjoy it."

She smiled and played her fingers along my hand. "Thank you for that. But, I lost everything, my house, my dignity, a lot of our friends, my business, everything. Emily had to move on to another place so she could afford to feed her family. And I had to do odd wedding kitsch jobs where I could. The Wilder place saved me."

"You saved us," I corrected. "I'm sorry about your grandmother."

"Thank you," she whispered and wiped away a tear. "And that's enough of that. I'm okay. I'm building up. I'm saving again since Clint took out our savings."

"Are you fucking kidding me?" I growled.

"No. He pretty much took everything, and the courts let him because I got screwed, and I didn't hire a good enough lawyer."

"We're going to make sure you have a good enough lawyer for anything else you need from now on."

"Thanks for that. I'm not going to let myself get into that position. Not again. Especially because I have a better lawyer now thanks to the trust—Clint isn't getting any of that. No matter what he thinks, he's not getting any of that."

The hairs on the back of my neck stood on end, and I frowned. "Why would you think that?"

She shook her head. "It's nothing."

"Really?"

"I'm just talking to myself now, but really, talk to me about you. That's enough about me."

"There isn't much about me," I said, letting the subject change for now.

"Um, excuse me, this is a date. You're supposed to tell me everything. Bare your soul to me." She grinned as she said it, and I just rolled my eyes.

"Let's see, I joined the Air Force right out of high school, and did it through the Air Force Academy because my father was able to get me in."

"What do you mean?"

"I had good enough grades, but you also need a recommendation to get in. It's a long, drawn-out process, and some people don't need it. Some people can just get in on their own merits, but I needed the boost, and my dad had a good friend to get me in. And it was the best thing I ever did in my life."

"Really?" she whispered.

"Really. I know some people don't like it, or only need it for a few years to find their path, but I loved it. I loved the order. I loved fighting for my country. I loved protecting people. I loved making sure that the guys that were younger than me coming in had a path."

"That's nice. I mean, I didn't really think about exactly what goes on, beyond what you hear in the news."

"And it's not what you read in the news, not completely. We're not just the nameless faces or faceless names. I trained, and I was good at what I did. I did my twenty, and then I needed something to do. I had always figured I would go back and work as a GS for the Air Force anyway. That's the civilian side."

"I know what a GS is because I live in San Antonio. It's the pay scale for civilians that work for the military and there are levels. There's more than one base around here. You get used to it since the military loves their acronyms."

"Good, not everyone else does. But I always assumed that's what I'd be doing. And then my sister lost her husband on deployment."

"Oh Eli, I'm so sorry." She squeezed my hand again, and I ran my thumb over her knuckles.

"I didn't really get to know him. My sister's much younger. But I watched her breakdown after not even being really able to know him because he was gone all the time. Other things went along with that, things that aren't my place to tell, but I needed to get out. And I needed to bring my brothers together, and I couldn't do that working for someone else. Evan got hurt, then Everett, and then something happened with Eli and East. All of it. Elijah has his own reasons for getting out, but I was the only one that stayed for my twenty, and the rest of them got out when their enlistment was up, and within a year, we were able to make it work here."

"And now you all work together, and live in the same place, for the first time in years."

161

"For the first time in twenty years," I whispered.

"That's insane," she whispered, shaking her head.

"I know. But I did what I had to for my family, and I don't regret this. Well, sometimes I do."

"Really?"

"Of course, I regret doing this sometimes. It's insane. Evan is the only person out of all of us with any semblance of connections to wine because of our uncles, so he fits in, even though he says he doesn't. East is doing what he does best, and the rest of us just filled in. We're making it work, we have the degrees, and we're gaining the experience, but we're literally following along the path of another chief master sergeant and another military man and his family."

"Was a good path. The people before you that owned that land knew what they were doing."

"So, I guess I sure as hell better figure out what I'm doing."

"And you will. I promise."

"Okay, that is enough of that. What do you say we finish our drinks and then head home?"

"It's an early night, Eli. We both have work in the morning."

I saw the heat in her gaze and swallowed hard.

"Yeah, early," I whispered, and did my best not to

swallow my tongue as she leaned forward and brushed her lips to mine.

"Oh fancy seeing you guys," a familiar and unwelcome voice said as I turned to see Brayden walking by, a beautiful woman with dark skin, bright eyes, and a sweet smile on her face at his side.

"Brayden," I said slowly. "Good to see you out." A total lie.

"Catalina, these are my archrivals, Eli and the beautiful Alexis. The wedding planner at their establishment."

"I've heard so much about you," Catalina said as she waved softly.

"It's nice to see you here. We were actually just heading out," Alexis said, her professional smile in place. I envied her that she could do that so easily.

"Of course, of course. It's good to see that the Wilders are doing well enough to enjoy a place like this. Moving up in the world."

Catalina frowned at that, and I had to wonder what a sweet girl like her was doing with a man like him, but it wasn't my place. For all I knew, Brayden wasn't an upstart dumbass. However, I wasn't going to think about it.

Brayden nodded at us, walked away with his date, and I looked at Alexis, who just shook her head.

"We are not letting him ruin this night."

"Good. Because I want to go on another date with you. I'm just saying."

"Oh. Good to know."

I grinned, leaned forward, kissed her again, and told myself that once again, this wasn't a mistake because it couldn't be.

"It's an early night, Eli. But yes, I'd like to do this again. I feel like we're just getting started."

I grinned at her wide eyes as if she hadn't meant to say that and nodded. "Sounds like a plan to me, because I want to know you, Alexis. And I sure as hell want to kiss you again."

Chapter Ten

Alexis

I swore my lips still tingled from the night before as I went through my day, doing my best to focus on work, on my wedding couples, and my distributors. Yet, all I could do was remember the scent of Eli. The scent I shouldn't be thinking about, and yet it was right there. Etched onto my skin and into my memories forever.

How could I still recall his taste after only a few kisses? We hadn't done anything beyond that, both of us knowing that we had other complications in the way.

But it was hard not to want more, to wonder who we could be if we just tried.

I shook my head and focused on my work. I had six weddings on the books and seven more consultations to see if I would be able to schedule them later in the next year. I only had certain days of the month for weddings, as others were booked for Elliot and his events. He didn't have as many as I did, though, at least when it came to the big rooms. He worked mostly on the smaller events with small groups.

But for now, I got to work with some of the most wonderful couples I have worked with so far.

Luke and Tracy were first, and they wanted a Cinderella ball on the ranch. Well, at least Tracy did, and Luke went along with it because he had stars in his eyes when he looked at her.

We had worked with a local ranch that wanted to get into the business, and we were going to have an actual horse-drawn carriage for the event. I couldn't help but smile, and I knew that a Cinderella ball on a European villa smack dab in the middle of South Texas was going to be a treat. But it was going to work.

Colin and Adam wanted a classic farm wedding that was going to put anybody else's social media to shame if I had anything to say about it. Emily and I were having a blast with the two guys picking out the perfect shades of purples and grays to go on the large picnic benches that we were going to use as the main table. We were going to put ten of them in a row, with a large runner and individual place settings. It was going to look gorgeous and slightly full.

Justin and Hannah wanted elegant French on a ranch. When they'd first told me that, I'd been puzzled for a moment, but I realized that with the architecture of the villa and the white pavers that created their own design in the middle of the entrance, we could make this work. It was going to be slightly Parisian, slightly ranch, but it was going to blend if I had anything to say about it.

Lucinda and Harvey wanted a classic small wedding and just wanted a space that all of their family could visit. They weren't inviting many people outside of their family, so they would take up just a few of the guest rooms, not all of them like a couple of the weddings that we were planning. They just wanted happiness, roses, and a space to be with one another. And I was going to make that happen.

Sabrina and Emily were having a full-on pink and *pink* rose wedding. Each of the girls had picked their own dresses, and they were white, fluffy, full trains of and lace and glitter, and I loved them. They weren't allowed to show each other, but it was my job to make sure they complemented one another, as they had told me if they picked the same dress or if they picked something that clashed with one another that I had to step in.

But these two loved each other and knew each other enough that their huge big wedding with all the pink roses was going to complement each other perfectly.

Matthew and Parker were having their huge Greek wedding, in Texas, of course. So there were going to be tons of Greek desserts and meals on Kendall's shoulders, including three cakes, and I was having a lot of fun doing my research with the matriarch of the family to ensure that we had their perfect wedding. It was going to be a huge family affair, and it was the last one on my books so far.

The first one was coming up soon, and it would be our showcase. The Wilder brothers, of course, had had other weddings, and they had gone fine, but we wanted the area to know we were here, to put our stamp on it. And that was my job.

Revved up by going through my notes, I rolled my shoulders back and realized I would be late for my girls' night if I wasn't careful. Maddie had scheduled this girls' night after she had heard about my date with Eli, and I knew the timing wasn't a coincidence. They wanted to find out what happened. I wasn't going to have too many details for them since it was just a lovely evening, with a little bit more deep dark secrets than I had planned to share, and wonderful kisses. And an awkward encounter, but that was fine. We seemed to be having a lot of those with the Dodge family.

However, Maddie and Kendall were going to have questions, so I would have to decide how much I would divulge when it came to my date and my upcoming second date with a certain Wilder brother.

I shook my head, grabbed the two gift bags that I had made for them, each containing a special notebook and pens that I loved, and headed towards the front door. I opened it in time to see someone ready to knock and nearly dropped the bags at the sight of him.

Clint stood there, a small smile on his face and eagerness in his gaze that he banked quickly to turn into something far more contrite.

"What are you doing here?" I asked, my voice shaking despite the months apart. I was far enough away from the rest of the resort so no one would be able to hear me. However, I just realized that nobody would be able to hear me scream if Clint did something. Not that he had ever done something, but I just realized how alone I was in this little area. And that was a lovely thought.

"I just wanted to see you. I told you we need to talk." He gave me that cajoling smile that I ignored for so long and hadn't seen the edges of until it was almost too late, and I wanted to slam the door in his face. Only, I couldn't because he would just keep coming back. Not always rudely, no, he would come back with a smile, and others would tell me to give him another chance. To say that he didn't mean to be such a dick for so long. Then he'd beat down my emotions and remind me I was nothing.

From the moment he had proposed at a wedding, I should have known that things were going to end poorly.

"Clint. I don't have time to talk to you."

"Are you off to a party then?" he asked as he looked down at the gift bags in my hand. "I see they're working you all hours of the night again if you're just now starting the day."

I gritted my back teeth together and told myself that I wasn't going to punch anybody. Barely.

"Clint. Please. I've asked you to leave politely, so you need to go." I could remember his screaming, the sneer on his face when he took everything. I needed him to go.

"Now, Alexis, is that really how you want to start things off?"

Finally the anger slid through the pain. "There is no starting. Only ending. Just stop. Really. You don't need to be here. We're divorced. You have everything that you've ever wanted, Clint. And that wasn't me, and I'm fine with that. But I have things to do, and you don't get to be here."

He raised his chin. "Now, Alexis. You really don't want to anger me like you used to."

Fear settled over me, but then I pushed it away, knowing it wouldn't help. "Don't demean me. Don't pretend. Just go."

"I just wanted to say that I'm sorry."

I blinked, shaking my head. "What? No, never mind. Just go."

"I'm sorry for the way things worked out. For how I acted. It was immature of me. I wanted to apologize and see if we could start on a different foot. One where I'm not the asshole."

I just looked at him, confused. This was a new one. Usually, he was saying what I owed him, even as he smiled through those big teeth of his.

"Clint, I appreciate you saying that though I don't know where it's coming from, however, I have places to be, and it's over. It's been over for a while. So you need to go."

"We should still talk, Alexis. We don't have to be enemies."

He had taken everything from me. My home, my business, my reputation, and my heart. What else was there? And this, on the day where all I had been doing was thinking about Eli's kiss.

I should just walk away and pretend that everything was fine, even when it wasn't.

"Goodbye, Clint." I closed the door behind me, locked it, and walked past him, careful not to touch him. He sighed, then headed down the path the other way. I shook my head, making my way to the winery so I could meet the girls.

I rubbed my temples, wondering what on earth that man could want. He had already taken everything from me, and now he wanted to annoy me.

He had also walked away when I asked him, it might have taken eight times, but he had.

Maybe that was progress.

Or maybe I was losing my damn mind.

I walked into the winery tasting room area and gave a polite smile to the small group with Maddie's cohorts and the vintner, and a few other people from the winery that I didn't know. When the Wilder's had bought the land and the companies on it, they'd already had all of their managers, and cellar masters, and vineyard masters in place.

The vintner, or winemaker, had been working for the company for twenty years, longer than the owners before the Wilders had even been here. I nodded at him as he spoke with a few wine club enthusiasts and made my way to the employee tasting room, where I would be with Maddie and Kendall again. It was nice that no matter who the owners were, that the winemakers and the people who had been on staff here for years had still found a home. The Wilders hadn't kicked them out. Instead, like with the customer service arm of the company, they had blended in, done their best to improve without harming. They hadn't fired anyone, but let those that wanted to leave in a huff go. They had tried to find their way as a family and as bosses while still keeping the reputation of a pretty damn good bottle of wine intact.

A pretty damn good bottle that I was going to need.

I practically stormed into the tasting room, and Kendall turned, a plate of hors d'oeuvres in her hands. "Okay, I'm glad that Maddie opened the wine. What is with you? Are you okay? What's wrong?" She set down the mushroom caps and pastries and came to me, gripping both hands. "What is it? Is it one of the brides? A staff member? That's got to be a Wilder."

I shook my head, pulled away slightly so I could hand her one of the bags. "I do need a glass of wine, so thank you, Maddie, for opening it."

Maddie bounced in, handed me a glass, same as Kendall, and I handed her a bag.

"Before I talk about it, let's make a toast."

"Sounds good to me," Maddie replied with a nod. "To figuring out what the hell is going on with us."

Kendall snorted but clinked glasses with us, then I took a sip of the pinot noir. It settled on my tongue, and I tried to breathe the same way that Maddie did, tasting. However, I just liked wine. I wasn't the connoisseur that Maddie was, or even Kendall.

"Yummy," I said. "Hints of oak?" I asked with a hollow laugh.

"As the red wine is stored in oak barrels, and our white in steel, yes, there probably is a hint of oak, but thanks for trying," Maddie said with a laugh. "And thank you for this," she said. She looked into the bag. "Oh, these notebooks are so cute."

"I love it. I take it you have a matching one then?" Kendall asked, and she picked up the notebook that I had personally chosen for her.

"All three of them are from the same line, but each to fit our needs. You know me and planning."

"Oh yes, I'm going to love it."

"I always liked taking notes, even if I'm not the big planner like you guys are," Kendall said with a laugh. "And I do taste that hint of oak." She winked as she said it, and we all sat down on the big couch in the corner, knowing that others could show up at any time, but that was fine. I wasn't sure what I would do if Eli Wilder showed up. So, I was going to pretend that I wasn't thinking about him.

"Now, as I gorge myself on these flaky savory pastries, you're going to tell me what is going on," Maddie ordered, as she did indeed bite down into a pastry and moaned like she was having an orgasm on the couch.

I popped one into my mouth and joined in her moan, and Kendall just beamed.

"You know, it's that sound that makes it all worth it. It's been so long for me. It's the only sound I'm getting," she added drily, and I nearly choked.

"Oh good, so we're going to jump right into the sex talk," Maddie said as she clapped her hands. "Now, first tell us what's going on, and then tell us about the date. And the sex."

I laughed; I couldn't help it. This is exactly what I needed, even if I hadn't realized it.

"It's not anyone other than my ex-husband who just showed up in front of my house to say we needed to talk and wouldn't leave."

"Is he still there?" Kendall asked while narrowing her eyes. "I can call Evan, or anyone," she corrected herself quickly, and I did my best not to look over at Maddie at the slip-up. "Seriously, I can call the cops."

"No, he's gone. He went down the path back to his car while I made my way here."

"Why was he there at all?" Maddie asked.

"Probably to see if we can get together so he can get my money." I rolled my eyes as I explained about my grandmother as I had the night before, and both girls reached out and gripped my hands, and I leaned into them, liking the idea that I had friends to talk to. I had Emily, of course, and she knew most of it, but Emily had her own family, and Emily worked for me. It was hard to show all of my weaknesses to someone who relied on me for their income. It was a weird dynamic, but these women didn't rely on me for anything. Other than friendship, at least I hoped.

"What an asshole," Kendall growled. "We can tell the Wilders that he's not allowed on the property."

"The property's too big for that, and I don't want to be in the center of anything. He's not going to show up again."

"I hope he doesn't," Maddie said softly. "But if he does, you need to tell one of the guys."

"I will. Maybe."

"You can at least tell Eli," Maddie hedged. "You know, since you went on a date and all."

"That's a beautiful segue," Kendall laughed. "But really, how'd the date go?"

I sighed dreamily this time, and the girls gave each other a look before clinking glasses together.

"The date was wonderful, the food was great, drinks were even better," I said with a laugh as Kendall snorted. "But the conversation was perfect. And oh my God, the way he kisses? Damn."

"Be still my heart," Maddie said with a laugh as she fanned herself, and Kendall just smiled softly.

"I guess it runs in the Wilder genes," Kendall whispered, and I pressed my lips together so I wouldn't ask any questions. It was weird knowing that Kendall had been married to one of the Wilder brothers, and none of us really talked about it. But we knew that Kendall wasn't ready yet. I hoped one day soon she will be, though.

"And, so, what happened after?" Maddie asked, leaning forward.

"That was it. We kissed, and then we went home."

"That's disappointing," Maddie shook her head. "Not even like a quick spiel or anything?"

I laughed, shaking my head. "Just a delicious kiss. And a promise for another date."

"Yay!" both women said at the same time, clinking their glasses together again.

"Y'all are incorrigible."

"Of course we are," Kendall said as she rolled her

shoulders back. "Either way, I'm happy for you. Eli's a good man."

"It's not going to get too serious," I corrected.

Maddie frowned. "Why?"

"Because I'm just getting out of a marriage that went to hell that's still annoying the fuck out of me. My ex-husband just showed up today, and here I am talking about dating my boss?"

"First, he's not your boss. Second, Clint has nothing to do with Eli," Kendall corrected.

"I made a bad choice before. I don't want to do it again and lose what I'm building here." I shrugged, but Maddie reached out and gripped my hand, even as Kendall continued.

"As someone who is literally working with her ex-husband, I can tell you that whatever mistakes you make here are not going to change what's happening with this business and with this group." Kendall gave a tight nod as my eyes filled with tears. "And don't cry. You don't need to cry over this. Eli's a good man. And you're going slow, so glacially slow that you've only kissed," she added dryly, and that made me laugh.

"I just don't know."

"You can't use Clint as the yardstick," Maddie added.

"I don't want to do that, but it's going to happen."

"Then try. I mean, it's hard not to, I understand, but try. Because you deserve that, as does Eli," Maddie whispered.

I nodded, took another bite of pastry, held back my moan this time, and looked between my two new friends and figured that maybe I could try, although it wasn't going to be easy.

We changed topics to work, of course, and wine, as Maddie brought out another bottle so we could taste it, this one a recently bottled Wilder, which tasted amazing. The grapes were a blend and settled right on my tongue. Maddie took notes, as did Kendall, and I felt like I should do the same, but I was happy to see that they were using their notebooks.

We were just cleaning up when there was a commotion outside, someone shouting, and I frowned as I ran after Kendall, Maddie on my heels as we made our way outside.

"Oh my God," I whispered as I looked at the red paint splattered on the side wall of the winery, and the dirt on the ground from where someone had dug up the flowers, then poured more red paint on the black mulch.

I blinked, trying to understand what I was seeing, but there was nothing cohesive. Just destruction.

And I looked at the girls, and at the poor guest who had seen it and had screamed, and went straight into work mode, knowing that something was wrong, and the Wilders were going to have to fix it, but I could do my job.

"Here, come here, I'm so sorry that this happened," I said quickly to the woman as she shook, staring at the wall.

"It looked like blood. I'm sorry for screaming."

"No, you alerted us something was going on," Kendall added as she looked over my shoulder. "And, here comes to cavalry. The Wilders are going to help us fix this up, and we're going to make sure that you're okay."

"I'm fine," the guest said. "It just startled me, that's all."

"We're going to make sure that we figure out exactly who did this."

"Probably kids, right?" the woman said as she shook her head, pulling her hair back behind her ears.

I met Kendall's gaze, then Maddie's, as the Wilder brothers ran up, and I told myself it had to be kids.

Because I didn't want to think about who else it could be.

Chapter Eleven

Eli

My feet hit the pavement at the sound of the first scream. Since I knew Alexis and the others were hanging out at the employee tasting room at the winery today, my heart raced, knowing where that scream had come from.

East was at my side, with Everett and Elijah running from the other side. Elliot was coming from the south, with Evan slowly coming behind him. Evan was moving pretty quick, but he had just had a fitting that morning and was in pain. Damn it, Evan needed to stay back. There was no way that I was going to make him. Not when Kendall was in the building where that woman had screamed.

I moved to Alexis' side first as the others came, everyone speaking at once. I met her gaze. "Are you okay?" I asked, knowing that I was acting not like the man that owned Wilder Resorts but rather the man who had just been on a date with her.

"I'm fine. As is Sasha." I looked down at the woman that was by her side, her eyes wide, and swallowed hard. "Mrs. Michaels. I'm so sorry."

"I'm sorry. I didn't mean to scream like that. I just thought it was blood."

I frowned at her words, then finally looked over their shoulder at the wall, at the dirt and the red paint everywhere. Plants and flowers had been dug up, and red paint had been splashed all over the bushes, pavement, tile, and white stucco.

I held back a curse, knowing that people were watching, waiting, and met Everett's gaze.

Everett nodded tightly, then whispered to East, who moved back towards the utility shed.

I shook my head at once. "We need to call the police, even though it's going to cause a scene, we need to."

My brothers all looked at me, except for Evan, who only had eyes for Kendall, but they all nodded, understanding.

. . .

It took an hour, all of us moving as one to keep guests out of the way and talk to the police. They sent two officers out to speak with us and the girls, but there wasn't much we could tell them. We couldn't tell them who we thought it could be. Was it kids? Dodge and his sons?

I didn't think they would sink this low. They liked taunting us, not doing something so blatant. That would be beneath them. At least I thought so.

Under the corner of my eye, I saw Kendall and Evan growling at one another before she stomped away, and he did the same. When she turned over her shoulder to look at him, I knew she wanted to reach out, to help him, but she wouldn't.

Because, God forbid, the two would have to talk to each other.

They walked away from each other, the cops did too after taking photos, statements, but I didn't think there was anything we were going to be able to do.

Maddie and Alexis had walked off with Mrs. Michaels, our guest, and I knew that Naomi would be around soon to make sure that she wouldn't have to pay for her stay and get anything else she wanted from us. She wasn't asking for it, but I wanted her to celebrate her time here with her husband.

"Word's going to get out," Evan growled at me as he came to my side. I looked at him then, the pain in his eyes, but I didn't ask because my brother would not appreciate it if I did.

"Yeah. It is."

East leaned forward. "What do you think's going to happen?"

Evan let out a breath. "Elliot will help Naomi spin it somehow."

My brows winged up. "Is that Elliot's job now? The publicist?"

Evan shrugged. "No, but he always has good ideas."

I looked over at Evan, at the anger in his gaze. "You're right. He is good at that. Fuck, who would do this?"

"Word is that Alexis' ex-husband was walking around here before. So was Brayden."

I cursed under my breath. "What do you mean her ex-husband was here?"

East snorted. "Notice he didn't latch on Brayden's name."

"No, I didn't. Because I assume Everett and Elijah are probably already dealing with him. Why the hell was Clint here?"

Evan tilted his head. "That the bastard's name?"

I glared. "It is. I don't want him on our property."

"We can keep him off, but only if she wants," Evan sighed. "You don't want to get in the middle of that."

"I will get in the middle of it if he's the one who did this."

East cleared his throat. "We don't know. The cops will tell us."

"And you're so good about waiting for the authorities to tell us?"

My brother looked at me then shook his head. "We had to take orders for all our lives, had to make sure we trusted those in charge. We can trust the cops to do this."

"You're right." I let out a breath.

"They're solid. They'll get it done. I just don't like the fact that the girls were alone in the building tonight when this happened."

"I don't like it either. Not that I can actually tell Kendall what to do."

I shook my head. "No, you can't. She wouldn't appreciate it. So, what are you going to do about it?"

"Nothing. She's going to drive home alone. And I'm not going to follow her like a fucking sucker."

"Good, because I don't want to have to bail you out of jail."

"Something going on between them?" I asked.

Evan snorted. "I don't think so. Not everybody wants to bang a staff member."

"Of all people here. You don't need to talk about that."

Evan snorted. "Touché, brother. Touché. And go get your woman."

"You said she was off with the others. I'll get her soon. I need to get calm before I see her."

"If she can't take you at your worst, then you're no good for her."

"Advice? Really?"

My brother just shook his head. "You're right. Shouldn't take advice from an old man who now works with his ex-wife and can't even be in the same room with her."

"Evan. What the hell happened between the two of you?"

I had never asked. This whole time, I had never asked. When my brother looked at me then, he just shook his head. "Mistakes were made. That's in the past."

"Evan, that's a lie."

East looked between us, silent as always, his own problems in his gaze.

"Maybe. But it's a lie that I'm going to learn to live

with. And the one you're going to have to learn to live with too."

I sighed but knew there was no reason I should keep going with that line of thought. Not when my brother would just resent me if I did.

I met with my other brothers and most of the guests, who had only heard some of the commotion, but we had made sure that we told them that we thought it was just kids playing a prank, and while it wouldn't be tolerated, we were happy to be welcomed into the neighborhood with such glee.

Even though we had been here over a year now, two years since we had signed the dotted line, we were still the newbies in this part of Texas, youngins.

Most people waved it off, and nobody left, asked for a refund, or said that they would never be gracing our doorstep again, and I had to count that as a win.

I made my way to my office with a sigh and figured I could head upstairs to my place or just stay here and work for a bit. I had endless paperwork. Even if Everett figured he could handle most of it, I had just as much as he did. The place was constantly in need of things. I hadn't been certain it could work. In the back part of my mind, part of me also needed it to. Because I needed my brothers to have a home. And we were making it. Slowly.

But fuck, who the hell had done this?

There was a knock at my door. I looked up, ready to growl at one of my brothers invading my space, but I didn't do anything, just in case it was a guest or Naomi.

When Alexis peeked her head in, I blinked, my throat going tight.

I stood up sharply, banged my knee against my desk, and cursed.

"Are you okay?" she asked, closing the door behind her.

She ran towards me, and I held my hand up. "I'm fine. I was having a shitty night. But probably not as shitty as you. Are you okay?"

She'd only come partway into the office, and as I met her halfway, I cupped her face, unable to hold back. I need to touch her. Hell, I had needed to touch her all damn day, but I had done a very good job about staying out of her way. As if I was afraid if she noticed that we spent too much time together, she would fucking run.

Which was probably the problem.

There wasn't time to breathe, so I tried to make that time. And possibly at the detriment of what we could be.

And look at me, becoming the man who actually cared about who I could be with another person, rather than what I could pretend to not to want at all.

I traced my fingers along her chin and let out a breath, letting my hand fall. "Alexis?"

"I'm okay. Are you? That had to be a shock to see your building hurt like that."

"To be honest, I was more afraid that you were in it. Hurt."

"Eli," she whispered.

I let out a breath, then began to pace, my hands at my side. "I don't know who it could have been. One of the Dodge kids? I don't think so. Did they hate us this much?"

"They always seem to lurk around," she mumbled, and my lips twitch. "I take it you heard about Clint?"

My shoulders tensed, and I turned to face her. "I did. Why didn't you tell me he showed up?"

She blinked at me, and I figured I had said the wrong thing, but I was genuinely curious. "Because it had nothing to do with you. I'm sorry, Eli, if that hurts you. But I didn't think it mattered. And I know that was the wrong thing to say, and I'm just so fuzzy right now I'm just not making any sense."

I sighed and moved forward, shaking my head. "You're right. It does have nothing to do with me."

"That's not how I meant it. What I was trying to say is like he's my ex-husband. It should have been part of my past, not part of my present. It should have been something that we talked about at dinner last night, and then I never had to talk about it again, but then he showed up saying that he was sorry or some shit, and I told him to leave, and he did. He left, Eli. And he was gone. I don't think it was him, but now the cops will talk to him, and now I'm going to have an issue with that, and what if it was Clint? I brought it to the Wilder's. What if I caused this trouble?"

I cursed again and then cupped her face. "If it was Clint, then he's the one who brought it. Not you. And if it was the Dodge brothers, then they did it. Not us."

"Good, tell yourself that. Because it is not your fault as the eldest Wilder that something happened tonight. No matter what happened, no matter who did it or the reasons behind it, it was not your fault."

My lips twitched, and I took a step back. "Damn you and your reverse psychology."

"It's not reverse if I'm just throwing it back at you." She paused. "Or maybe it is. I'm drained, and I only had two glasses of wine, and I wanted more, and then things just got insane."

"Was it good wine?"

She grinned then. "It's Wilder Wine. Of course it was good wine."

I laughed then. "Evan's the one with the nose for wine. And I just assume we make kick-ass wine because we're Wilders, and we wouldn't do anything bad."

"Are you kidding me? You don't know your wine? And you own a winery."

"I'm learning my wine. Elijah and Evan are the ones that know their wine. The rest of us are just catching up. Which makes me sound like a dumbass for buying this place, but each of my brothers went to the position that they most likely were to fit in."

"You guys are doing a great job."

"Not sure about that. Especially not tonight."

"Eli. I'm sorry that tonight ended as it did."

"You know, I was going to use your girls' night as an excuse to walk you to your door tonight. You know, to make sure you made it home okay."

Her lips twitched, and she went to her tiptoes, kissing me softly. I groaned into her, needing that taste, the slight pinot noir on her lips, but the clearness in her gaze.

"Well, I think I would have let you walk me home."

"If only, right?"

In answer, she moved back, leaving me feeling a little disappointed, before she stepped back softly, one step, then another, and locked the door with a click behind her.

I raised a single brow and growled. "Well then."

191

"What? I just don't want to be interrupted."

"For what exactly?"

"I don't know, why don't you tell me?"

In answer, I took two steps toward her, cupped her face, and kissed her hard. She moaned into me, and then we were tugging at each other, fast and quick, and all I wanted to do was strip her down to nothing, but this was our first time, and I wanted her to know that I wasn't a complete barbarian. Just a partial one.

Our tongues tangled as I slid my hands down her waist and cupped her ass. She rocked into me, her body soft against the hardness of my cock against her.

"Eli," she mumbled against me, and I kept kissing her, kneading. Heat spread between us, as the sounds of us against one another filled my office. I didn't care that this is where we worked because, fuck, I lived right above this, and she lived right behind the place. There was no escaping where we worked. We lived here, we ate here, we were going to fuck here.

I gently moved her towards my desk, but instead of sitting on top of it, I pushed her towards the thick leather chair. She groaned, sitting down, and I went to my knees in front of her. Her eyes widened as I knelt before her, sliding her skirt up slightly.

"Eli."

"I need to taste you."

She put one leg above my shoulder, the other pointed down onto the ground, as I spread her before me, pushing up her skirt. She wore little black lace panties that were glistening already. When I shoved them to the side, I nearly came in my pants. She was wet, hot. When I put my mouth on her, she just groaned, sliding her hand through my hair as I licked and I savored. Her thighs were around my shoulders as I ate her out, and the leather beneath her squeaked slightly. The scent of stale coffee and ledgers and leather filled the air, but all I could taste was the ambrosia of her pussy.

And when I slid two fingers in her and gently bit down on her clit, she came, orgasming around me, and she called out my name, nearly coming off the chair.

"Eli, I can't, I can't."

She couldn't finish her statement, but all I could do was keep touching, keep kissing, and when I stood up, I pushed her back on the chair slightly, cupping the back of her neck and crushing my mouth to hers. She groaned, smiling against me as our mouths tangled with one another, and then I moved back and gently pulled her out of a chair and lifted her onto the desk.

"We're going to break that computer," she laughed, but I shoved it to the side gently before I latched onto her mouth again. I pushed her shirt up, her bra down roughly, and she pulled at my pants, my belt, and then I was lowering my face down to her, kissing her breasts, sucking at her nipples, and she arched into me, taking me out of my pants. She pumped me, once, twice, squeezing my length, and both of us groaned.

"Condom. I need a condom."

"My purse," she mumbled, my eyes widened.

"From the date. I had it with me. Sue me."

"Oh, you're my favorite person right now. And I will be keeping condoms in here from now on."

"So this is going to be a regular occurrence then?" she teased as I scrambled for her purse, pulled out the condom, and slid it over my length.

"Oh, I'm going to fuck you right here, and I'm planning on doing again. Often. Because you all flushed and disheveled on top of my desk, where normally you are prim and proper Alexis? Fuck yeah."

She moaned, and then we kissed again, both of us reaching for each other. And when I slid deep inside her, and she stretched around me, I met her gaze, we both groaned, and time stopped.

Literally, right then, I could hear nothing, feel nothing. I could just see her and know that this was when things changed.

I wasn't this man. I wasn't the guy who looked into

the future beyond what I could do to save my family. And yet, right then, this was it. I knew it.

As I looked at her gaze, she was just as fucking scared as I was.

But I moved again, and again, and she arched into me, her legs wrapped around my waist, and I laved at her breast, kissed her hard on the mouth, and she dug into me, both of us groping for one another as we pushed papers off the desk, and moved against one another.

She came again, and I followed, groaning into her as her pussy clamped around my cock like a vice.

"Alexis," I growled into her throat, biting down.

"Eli."

And I knew there was no getting out of this. There was no walking away.

And I might've made a mistake before, but I wasn't going to make it again.

Not when it came to Alexis. And that in itself was something I was going to worry about. But not right now. Not when she was hot and wet around me, and all I could do was taste her on my mouth.

And so I kissed her again and went slower.

Hoping to hell I knew what the fuck I was doing.

Chapter Twelve

Eli

"You did what?" Everett asked.

I set down the boxes in my hands and shrugged, acting as if this was a normal conversation. "I invited Alexis to dinner."

"With us. In my cabin."

I snorted. "You don't have a cabin. You have a house. The biggest house on the property."

"True, because I was lucky when we were drawing straws. But that's beside the point. You invited a woman to our family dinner where we sit around and eat food and pretend that we're civilized?" he asked, his brows raised.

"He invited Alexis?" Elijah asked before reaching for his suit jacket that he had taken off when he had first walked in. He had been in meetings all day and had hadn't come quite as casually as everyone else, and I laughed, shaking my head. "I'm going to go pick her up."

"By walking. Because we all live together on this compound that couldn't be more incestuous," Evan growled as he rattled around in the kitchen. Elijah and Elliot were in there with him, cooking, while East was muttering outside on the deck fixing one of the planks.

I wasn't quite sure how this had become my life, how we all lived together, worked together, and now I was bringing a woman who happened to live and work with us to this dinner.

Yes, dating someone I lived with, worked with, and saw nearly every day was probably a mistake, but here I was, inviting her to dinner.

"I invited her after the whole incident with the property damage." I pinched the bridge of my nose and let out a breath. "She was freaked out, so I said she should come to dinner."

Elijah blinked at me. "Before or after you had sex with her in your office?" he asked casually as Everett snorted beside him.

I looked at my two brothers and glared. "Excuse me?" I asked in my most prim voice.

"Oh, you're not excused, because I heard everything," Elijah said with a grin.

I blinked. "What?" I asked, and I could feel the blood drain from my face.

"Okay, I guess I owe you ten dollars," Everett said with a sigh. "I thought that Elijah was wrong. But here you are, having sex in your office like you're on some sort of CEO show like that one with doctors who have sex in utility closest."

"What CEO show has sex in the office? No, I don't need details. It's not like I have time to watch TV. And the only show I can think of right now with sex in the office was the Oval Office, and that was years ago." I couldn't help but laugh as my brothers just shook their heads, handing over money.

"I didn't hear everything, don't worry, but I heard enough squeaks against the desk that I walked away quickly and made sure nobody came around that hallway. Which is a good thing because there were guests in the fucking building, Eli."

I narrowed my eyes. "Guests don't come down that hallway. Hell. Don't tell Alexis."

"Keeping secrets from your girlfriend already? Is that a good thing?" Everett asked, teasing.

"First off, fuck you. Second, I don't know if she's my girlfriend. We're still figuring this the fuck out, so stop trying to freak her out through me. And hell, stop trying to freak *me* out. Third, I've had sex in my place before, and that's in the same building as all these guests. And I damn well know that people have had sex in our guest rooms. And our cabins."

"I've had sex in this cabin," Elijah said with a grin.

I rolled my eyes. "Thanks, thanks for that image."

"Hey, at least you didn't have to hear the grunting and squeaking."

I blinked. "I thought you just heard the desk squeak."

"I might have lied, and I'm not telling you what I lied about." Elijah looked innocent, and I wanted to punch him, yet I knew I couldn't. Eliza would frown on that, and fuck, so would Alexis.

"So she's not your girlfriend. You're just fucking the wedding planner then?" Evan asked with a growl as he walked in, glowering.

I stared at my brother then, and I knew there was more happening here than just whatever he was saying. He and Kendall had fought about something else, and yet it wasn't as if when I asked, he would tell me. Because, God forbid, my brothers tell me what they were doing or feeling. Instead, we had all moved here,

199

and worked together, lived practically on top of one another, and I had no idea what anybody was doing because they wouldn't tell me.

"I thought it would be nice if Alexis had a home-cooked meal, okay?" I said, regretting my life choices in many aspects at this moment. "I realize that it was probably a mistake asking her to come here with you lot. However, you know her, you see her, and I assume you like her."

"Of course, we like her," Evan growled out.

"Good. You like her, and so do I."

"How much do you like her?" Elijah asked, and I nearly threw my phone at him.

"She has no family here, none in the fucking country, so I figured it'd be nice if she could just hang out with us. If that is too much, then I will take her out somewhere else. And hell, after the whole incident with the paint, it freaked me out. Freaked her out. I thought it would be nice if she could get to know us beyond those crazy Wilder brothers."

"I don't know if having a meal with us is actually going to help that sentiment," Everett put in.

I snorted. "True. Hell though, I figured why not try?"

"So, this is meeting the family members. It's very interesting," Elliot put in as he came forward.

I shook my head. "If it were 'meeting family members,' it would be meeting Eliza, and that would be a whole different situation."

My brothers gave each other a look, and then nodded, knowledge in their gaze.

Our parents weren't here with us anymore, so there would never be a meet the parents when it came to anyone that we dated or married. Not that I was planning on marrying Alexis. I need to get that thought out of my mind. However, Eliza was the closest thing we had to the matriarch of the family. She was our baby sister, so when we introduced her to someone we were dating, that's when we knew it was serious, just like when our baby sister introduced her husband to us.

That's when everything had changed.

Of course, we had sort of bombarded her to make that happen, so I wasn't quite sure it was the same thing.

"Go get her. We'll be on our best behavior."

I narrowed my eyes at Everett, who just shrugged, and then let out of yelp as Evan slid his arm around our younger brother's neck and dragged him to the kitchen. "I'll keep him in line."

Elijah just sighed. "And I suppose I will keep all of them in line."

"I do believe that's Evan's job."

"No, it's yours. But I'm glad you invited her. I like the way that you are around her."

I frowned, wondering where this was coming from. "You do?"

"Yes. What I know is that she's a good person and fits in with us. I suppose we'll see how much after tonight."

Alarm began to slide through me even though I knew his words were true. I'd felt that connection with Alexis the first time I saw her, even though I'd told myself it was insane to feel so right out of the gate. I was old enough now that I knew I wanted to settle down, but hell, I wasn't ready to let Alexis know my brain had already decided, and my heart was well on the way to following. "Don't make this as big of a thing as you're making it."

"No, I think you already did that."

I sighed and then left him in the house, hoping my brothers would get their shit together before I got back. Halfway down the path, I nearly ran into Alexis and blinked. "I thought I was picking you up at your house?"

She smiled up at me, and I couldn't help but push her hair back off her shoulder to lean down and kiss her neck. She shivered, then cleared her throat. "Don't you think that's rather silly? Considering it's not that much of a hike to Elijah's place."

"Maybe, but I was trying to go for some semblance of normal considering we're all in walking distance, although some of us more of a walk than others."

She just shook her head. "True, so, how about I walk with you the rest of the way back."

"That sounds like a plan." That's when I noticed she had a covered dish in her hand, and I reached forward, taking it from her. "You cooked for us?"

Her cheeks pinked, and I wanted to lean down and brush my fingers along them but refrained since my brothers were probably watching. "I baked a pie. I wasn't sure what you guys were having for dinner because I didn't ask, and we've been busy with everything else, but I had time to bake a cherry cobbler."

I practically drooled right then and went to take off the cover, and she slapped at my hand.

"Stop it. Not outside where a bug could get on it."

"Really? That's what you're worried about?"

"We're in Texas. The bugs are like three times as big as anywhere but Australia. Of course, a bug is going to come at us. They're constantly trying to attack me—that and frogs. Did you know once I was walking up the path to go meet a client and a frog hit me in the face?" she asked, her voice high pitched, and I snorted.

"You're serious?" She was so damn cute.

"Of course, I'm serious. I'm not going to make up a

frog slapping me in the face. It looked just as concerned as I was. It hopped away, looking all happy still, but it slapped me. A frog slapped me."

I pressed my lips together and tried not to laugh, but I looked down, seeing her narrow her eyes at me.

"I know you want to laugh. And I also know you want to laugh about the time that I tried to do some form of martial arts that I am not trained for to keep the wasp away from me."

The mental image filled my mind, and I grinned. "I did see that."

"There are so many bugs."

"We try to take care of them, but we also live in ranch country. In South Texas. Bugs and reptiles happen."

"I hope by reptile, you are not talking about an S-N-A-K-E."

"Did you just spell out snake?"

She waved me off, hushing me. "Don't say it out loud. You're going to call it."

"Like a pied piper for snakes?"

"Eli Wilder. If you say S-N-A-K-E one more time, I am walking back to my cabin down this path."

"Alone, where any S-N-A-K-E could come after you."

"You're mocking me, and while I believe I deserve it right now, I don't appreciate it."

I snorted, gripped her hand with my free one, and tangled my fingers with her. She looked up at me and blushed.

"Are you sure it's okay that I'm coming to family dinner?"

"Well, since we are right at the door, I hope so."

"Eli," she mumbled, trying to pull her hand back. I latched on tightly and squeezed.

"It's fine. I promise. They know you, Alexis. They like you. Come inside. They don't bite. Hard."

"You say that, and yet I'm pretty sure you're lying."

"Maybe, but they do like you. And it might be weird, but mostly just for me."

"Why would it be weird for you? Because we had sex in your office?" She whispered that last part, and I cringed.

"Not that part, but I should let you know that Elijah heard us. I was thinking about if I should tell you or not, but I don't want to start off whatever this is between us with a lie."

She blinked and paled. "Oh. That's good to know. I'm just going to go jump into this set of trees over here where I'm sure there's an S-N-A-K-E that can kill me."

"Alexis," I said with a laugh.

"It's fine. It's really fine. I'm just going to pretend that that didn't happen because we had sex, Eli. And now I'm here having a family dinner with you, with people that I work with. To say that this is complicated would be an understatement."

I met her gaze, still holding that pie, and leaned down and kissed her softly on the mouth. And just at that moment, I could breathe again. There was probably something wrong with that.

"It's going to be okay. We're adults. Not kids anymore. This isn't a college dance or us freaking out because we're in our twenties and feeling left behind. We've done this before. This is normal."

She rolled her shoulders back. "I've been married before. I can do this."

"I haven't been married before, but I have faced down an enemy while in an aircraft. I have thought I was going down before, thought I was losing it all. I think I can handle dinner with my family."

"Oh good, as long as we're putting those on the same level, I feel so reassured."

"Is he telling you about his nearly fell out of the sky story again?" Evan asked from the doorway with a huff.

"Maybe," I said with a laugh.

"Just asking. Is that a pie plate?" Evan asked, holding out his hands. "Give me."

I raised a brow. "No peeking, we don't want bugs."

"It's Texas. There are bugs," Evan said as he pulled the pie dish out of my hand. "I'll go stick it in the kitchen so it's away from the guys who will try to eat this pie before we have dinner."

Alexis leaned forward. "Well, good, it's cherry cobbler."

"Well, now I'm going to go stick this in my car," he said with a wink, sounding far lighter than I had seen him in a while. It was almost like he was the old Evan, but I knew that it wasn't real. He was acting the part, or at least pretending for Alexis' sake. So I had to count that as a win.

I shook my head as Evan walked away, leaving the door open, and gestured for Alexis to walk in.

The house was mania, as everyone was putting the food on the table, laughing at one another, music on, and it felt normal to me, six big guys who talked too loud, who were a little too big, and didn't know how to be quiet, but it was home.

In contrast, Alexis was around five-four, a tiny little sprite, but gorgeous as hell.

She winked at me and looked like the commander and planner that I knew she was.

"Hello boys, I brought pie. Make sure you get some after dinner before Evan steals it all."

"Narc!" Evan shouted from the kitchen, and she laughed.

"Just one pie?" Everett said with a sigh. "Next time, you're going to have to bring six. Just so you know the rules."

"I'm not making six pies for you guys. Sorry. At least unless it's a holiday."

"Well, we're just going to have to teach you," Elijah added with a wink as he gestured towards where they were sitting at the table.

"We're going with a lot of roasted meats, some sides, and a lot of bread. We have green beans there, so we have a vegetable, but we just wanted things to put gravy on."

Alexis looked around, and I squeezed her hand. "Seems like I came right at the right time."

"And I hope you're going to want wine because it's what you're getting," Elliot said with a wink as he handed over a glass of pinot noir. "This is your favorite, right?"

An odd sense of jealousy bubbled in me at the fact that Elliott knew, but those two worked together the most, so it made sense.

"You know I love anything wine."

"That's my type of girl," Elijah said with a grin as Evan huffed in and stared at the glass in her hand.

"That's the good vintage. I also have a rosé back there chilled because Elliott said you might like it."

"I'm going to get spoiled." She said with a laugh as she looked up at me.

I shook my head. "I don't know who these guys are. These are not the Wilder brothers I grew up with."

"Don't worry. We're going to start cursing more and scratching things soon," East put in and went to sit down. "Dinner got done a little quicker than I planned, so we better eat before it gets cold."

I looked down at Alexis, who in turn looked around at my brothers, and straightened. "I suppose if I want to get my plate, I should fight for it."

"It's the only way. We're Wilders," Everett stated before we all took our seats around the table, Alexis sitting closest to me, Evan on her other side.

Evan was back to glaring, staring at his phone, but none of us asked who it was. Instead, we piled our plates high, with the wine flowing and laughter ensuing as my brothers decided to make sure I was the center of the evening.

"Seriously though, he was completely naked, hanging out of the nearest window, and Mom just kept shouting that if he wanted to come inside, he better find his pants," East said with a laugh, and I just pinched the bridge of my nose.

"Do we have to tell this story?"

Elijah sighed. "We do. Because you were naked."

Alexis just beamed up at me. "I'm going to like this. Then I'll know all of your secrets."

I shook my head. "You shouldn't know my secrets. Especially not ones that involve being naked hanging out of a window."

"Eliza knows all of them. All of ours," Everett put in. "When you meet her, she's the one to ask."

"Oh, she's the one I haven't met, still sounds intimidating. Not that you guys aren't," she added quickly. "Why was he naked?"

I shook my head. "I don't want to talk about it."

Evan grumbled, but Elliot answered. "Because a girl that he had a crush on said that only the best guys sleep naked, so he was seventeen, sleeping naked, and grateful that he had his own room, and then had that lovely nightmare in which he tried to push his way out of the house."

"It's not my fault that I forgot that the windows were open since the AC was out, and we didn't have screens in that particular house," I grumbled.

"Oh my God, that's just too hilarious."

"And so I was hanging out of the window, my ass glowing in the moonlight, and my mother wouldn't let

210

me back in until I explained to her why I was naked and trying to sneak out."

"You terrorized our parents enough that by the time they got down to me, they knew all of the Wilder tricks. There was no way I could get by," Elliot said with a pout, and Alexis narrowed her eyes and shook her head.

"You know I don't believe that for a second, Elliot Wilder. You were the baby. Just like Eliza. I'm pretty sure you lived up to that Wilder name, and you got away with everything."

Everyone hooted with laughter, and I grinned. "Pretty much. He thought he wasn't getting away with much, but our parents had gotten a little laxer by the time they got to kid six and seven."

Alexis leaned into me, and everything felt right. There was probably a problem with that, but I ignored it. "I cannot believe your parents had so many. I still think that it was loud with just the two of us."

"It's always loud, and now that we all live near one another, it just gets louder," Everett said with a sigh, and Alexis smiled.

"Well, I'm glad I'm getting to know all of you. However loud you may be. Although I will have to say, next time, I'm going to have to bring extra pie."

She smiled up at me, and I tangled my fingers with

hers, wondering how the hell we had gotten here because this wasn't that dance at that wedding, this wasn't a kiss on a date or even a bare brush of skin against skin as we walked past one another in the hallway.

No, this was dinner with family. This meant something.

And I hadn't realized how much until now.

And I had no idea what I was supposed to do about it.

Chapter Thirteen

Alexis

I woke up to one hand on my hip and arched back into Eli, craning my neck just for a single touch. A single breath.

Eli did not disappoint.

The night before, we had worked on our perspective projects long after dinner and had tumbled into bed, laughing, doing our best to pretend that we weren't stressed out about what was happening today.

And had enjoyed each other, sliding along the sheets and tasting every inch of one another.

We had done all of this, all while dealing with a thousand other things during our day.

"Good morning," he mumbled before he bit down gently on my neck. I shivered and reached around me to grip him. He was hard and thick, and when he groaned, he rocked his hips into me. "That's one way to wake me up," he whispered before he licked where he had bitten.

"We both have meetings this morning, and today is the wedding."

The first wedding that I would be officially in charge of on the grounds. It had been weeks since I was hired, since I had moved here, weeks since I had met the Wilder brothers in truth. Months since my life had changed.

And a few weeks since I had first kissed Eli.

And now here we were, in bed together, acting as if this was our new normal.

I didn't want anything else, not at that moment. Because everything just felt right and comfortable, and of course, that scared me.

"We can be quick," he mumbled before he flipped me on my back and moved to the end of the bed. My eyes widened as he spread me before him and licked his lips. "I know what I'm having for breakfast."

I rolled my eyes and nearly laughed at him before he clamped his mouth on my pussy, and I shook, the feel of his warm mouth and very talented tongue over my clit nearly sending me over to the edge with just one touch.

And he pushed my thighs wider, his calloused thumbs roaming along the softness of my skin, and I moaned, arching into him as he lapped and sucked. He trailed his fingers along my inner thigh, over my pussy, and then he spread me wider before inserting his middle finger inside me. I clamped down around him, arching into his face, as he continued to suck and to lick, heat radiating from both of us.

The slight rubbing from his beard sent me over the edge right as he curled his finger. I came, just like that, riding his face, wondering how it had happened so quickly. How could this man do things to me so easily, without me even being aware he could do it?

Before I could say anything, before I could do anything, he flipped me over on my stomach, squeezed my thighs together, and spread my cheeks for him. I blushed, never having this much fun or this much freedom when in bed before. But this was Eli, he knew what he was doing, and he knew exactly how to get me off and to make me blush. He always liked it when I blushed.

He'd lowered his head again, licked me to near orgasm one more time before he played with me, and I arched up to him, going to my hands and knees as I looked over my shoulder. "If you don't get inside me now, I'm going to turn the tables and take you into my mouth."

He grinned. "I don't really think that that's a threat," he said with a wink, so I grinned, twisted slightly, and ended up in front of him, both of us naked, my breasts against his chest. He kissed me hard and I could taste myself on him. I slid my hand down between us and gripped him tightly.

"This is one way to wake up in the morning," I repeated, and he winked at me, sliding his hand along me, so he was playing with my folds. I pulled away slightly, even as he grunted, and bent in front of him, my fingernails digging into his hips as I took him into my mouth. He let out a groan that went straight to my core, and I sucked him down, humming along his length. I couldn't suck all of him. He was too big for that, but I could take most of him, hollowing out my cheeks as I did so. He grunted, his hips moving on their own, and I just smiled, grateful that I could get this reaction from him.

He kept moving, the saltiness of him settling over my tongue, and then he moved away again, nearly tossing me on my back, my breasts bouncing as we both laughed, and then his mouth was on mine, and he was between my legs. Both of us let out a shocked groan as he slid deep inside, and we froze.

"Fuck. I forgot a condom."

I blinked up at him, shocked as hell that I had forgotten as well.

I shook my head and tightened my legs around his hips. "I'm on birth control, and both of us were tested. Just in case. It's okay."

He looked at me then, his eyes dark. "You feel so fucking good with me bare inside you."

I blushed, even as my pussy clenched. "Good, now move. I need you to move."

"Anything you need. Anything." And he kept kissing me, moving in and out of me, to the point that I could barely breathe, barely think. This wasn't the first time that we had made love in his apartment. It wasn't the first time we had woken each other up like this. But this felt like a first time for something else, and I wasn't sure how I felt about it, how I was supposed to feel.

Because this was Eli. This was me. And why did everything feel like there was too much all at once?

But I pushed those thoughts out of my mind. I needed to be here right now. Because later, I would be working and focusing on everything else. I couldn't let myself drown, couldn't let myself fall. Because I had fallen once before, and it had been too much. This was just fun, just a moment in time.

Eli flipped us again, going on his back, so I rode him,

and he frowned at me. "All attention on me. On us. Get out of your head, baby."

I knew he was right, so I slid my hands over my breasts and rolled on him, continuing to move, knowing that if I weren't careful, I would fall for him, and I couldn't. Not again. I couldn't complicate the situation any more than it was. This was just for fun, and I had to remember that, no matter the cost.

He looked at me then, reaching up for me and pulling me down to him. I groaned and leaned down to kiss him as tears threatened. Tears that didn't need to be there.

So I wouldn't let them.

I continued to kiss him as my orgasm rocked through me, and he filled me, the wet heat between us something more than just sex, and that scared me.

Because everybody already knew what we were doing, they knew what happened when we were alone. And they all wanted something more than was already there. I was now the center of attention again, something I promised I would never be again, as the wedding planner was supposed to be in the background. So I would have to do better. Be better.

And when I finally blinked out of my own thoughts, Eli was frowning at me, even with the heat and emotion in his gaze that should worry me. "You weren't there with me for the last of that. What's wrong, baby?" he asked as he slid his thumb over my cheek.

I shook my head. "Sorry, I think I'm a little worried about work. You know."

He frowned at me but nodded. "I get that. But I'm still balls deep inside of you, so focus on me for a minute. I'm selfish."

That was the problem with Eli. He wasn't selfish. But I needed him to be. It was easier to pretend when he was.

"Sorry," I whispered, and then I leaned down to kiss him softly. He groaned into my mouth. My phone buzzed and I cursed. I slid off of him, a little embarrassed, and I looked down at my phone. "Damn it. It's the photographer texting. I have to get ready to go." I looked at the clock, cursed again. "I didn't realize it was so late. Even with our alarms."

"We're still ahead of time. I set another alarm for the last minute that we could be in bed. We haven't hit snooze yet. I'm not going to let us fuck up today. It's important."

I met his gaze, and I panicked. I *panicked*. This was important, and here I was lying in bed, sticky and gross after having sex with the man who wasn't my boss but was totally still my boss.

"I've got to go. I'm sorry."

I ran into the bathroom, cleaned myself up, got dressed as quickly as possible, even as I heard Eli curse and get ready in the bedroom.

"Alexis. What's wrong?"

"Nothing's wrong. It's just Tracy and Luke's wedding today. We have to make sure that we have everything ready. I need to go home and finish prepping."

"I thought you were going to get ready here this morning?" he asked, and I shook my head, even as I grabbed the bag I had brought over so I could indeed prep over here. It had seemed like such an easy thing to do the night before when he had suggested it, now it seems like far too much of a commitment. Far too much of a promise when this whole thing was supposed to be casual. This was Eli. A friend. Nothing more. We couldn't let it be more, or I would hurt him. Or he would hurt me, or it would just be too much.

I could feel myself begin to hyperventilate, but I threw my bag over my shoulder and shook my head. "I forgot a couple of things, and I have to be the perfect wedding planner today. But seriously, I'll see you soon." I went to my tiptoes, brushed a kiss on his lips, ignored the clutch in my belly because I wanted more, because I was scared to want more. I moved to walk away, to get home, and try to settle myself. Because I didn't want to hurt Eli, I didn't want to get hurt. And I just wanted things to be normal when I didn't know what was normal.

Eli reached out and gripped my hand. "Alexis. Talk to me."

I shook my head, then went to my tiptoes again to kiss him. "It's okay. I'm just a little stressed for the day. But we've got this."

He studied my face, and I was so afraid that he could read my thoughts. "We do. You've worked your ass off."

"So have you."

"Okay then. I'll see you at the wedding?"

My heart did that little clutch thing again, but I ignored it. "Yes. At the wedding."

I practically jogged down the hall and ran smack into Evan. He held my shoulders and looked down at me. "Are you okay? What's wrong?" He looked over my head and narrowed his gaze, and I pat him on the chest, moving back.

"I'm fine. Sorry. I'm just running late."

"You're not hurt?" he asked, and that right there was why it was hard to stay away from the Wilder brothers, because they were always there for you—always wanting to take care of you. I had to take care of myself. I learned the hard way what happened when I didn't.

"I'm fine. Really. And this is super awkward because you know exactly where I just came from."

He shrugged. "You're seeing my brother. You both look happy. Not quite sure why anything else would be my business."

I smiled up at him then and shook my head. "I guess you're right. Now I need to head out. I have to call back a couple of other people and meet with Kendall." He stiffened for a minute, and I pulled away. "Sorry."

"It's okay. I'm an adult. I can work with Kendall."

He didn't sound like he wanted to, but that was fine.

I made my way back to my house without seeing anybody else, as it was early enough in the morning that the sun was just now rising, and people were starting to wake up. I knew Kendall and Sandy were busy getting ready for the guests and their morning breakfast, as well as the fact that the bride and groom were in the honeymoon suite on the other side of the building.

They had spent the night together and hadn't wanted to go with tradition and not see each other this morning. However, soon they would be pulled apart and forced to spend a couple of hours away from each other while they each got ready.

They were adorable, and this whole Cinderella farm ranch thing that they wanted was going to be beautiful.

I could already see the team working on flowers and

other things on the other side of the tiled walkway, and I nodded tightly, doing my best not to freak out. I showered quickly, put my hair up in a small chignon at the base of my neck, put on a dove gray dress and coat, and called myself okay for the day. I slid my feet into my heels, grateful for the comfort pads I had put at the balls of my feet so I wouldn't end up with blisters at the end of the day.

I fielded call after call from my team, the bride, the bride's mother, the ranch that was delivering the horses, and countless other people. Because I was not only working on Tracy and Luke's wedding today, I also had the other five weddings, eight now, if I counted the one we had signed for later next year to deal with. But between Emily and me, we had it handled.

And I was just going to not worry about the fact that I had woken up in Eli's bed and it had felt like home.

I ran into Maddie on my way back in, and she handed over a mug.

"Is this coffee?" I asked, my mouth going dry.

"It's a coffee protein shake. You can have coffee after you eat this."

I blinked. "What?" I asked.

"Kendall handed it to Emily, who handed it to me because I was coming this way. Now eat, be happy, and you can do this. I've heard amazing things about your other weddings. This is just one more event."

I snorted, even as I took a sip, and groaned at the yummy taste of it. Kendall was a genius. "Um, no. This is not just a normal wedding. This is my first Wilder wedding."

"And you need to be the backbone. Because I know that these brothers are stressed the fuck out too."

I nearly tripped. "What?"

"Of course, they're stressed out. They've done weddings before, well, at least the other wedding planners have on the property, but it's different now. Because they really want this to work. Because you're one of them."

I grimaced. "Because I work with them. I'm not one of them."

Maddie's eyes widened. "Okay. We're going to just dissect that later, with Kendall. Maybe even Naomi, if we can drag her away from her man."

I shook my head. "We don't have time for that."

"Right now, no, we don't. But we are going to talk about it. Because you seem to be running."

"I'm not running."

I was indeed running in my heels, but I didn't care.

"We're going to talk about it!" she called out from

behind me, and I waved her off and put my earphone in so I could call Emily.

I met with the florist, the photographer, went over a few more things with Kendall and her team, but we were on track. I wasn't going to say that out loud, but I did allow myself to at least think it.

The officiant would be showing up soon, and we'd had the rehearsal the night before in the barn, and everything had gone off without a hitch. Even the three flower girls and three-ring bearers had done admirably. I wasn't going to worry about the fact that everything could change on a dime today, but it was fine. Everything was going to work out.

And I kept that on a mantra in my head as I waved at the father of the groom and the mother of the bride. They were having a heated discussion, but it seemed to be about a hockey team and not about the wedding as I walked by.

"You look wonderful," the mother of the bride said as she waved at me.

I smiled. "Thank you. You look wonderful as well."

"I'm so glad that you talked me into this dress, rather than something a little more matronly," she said with a grin as she looked down at her simple yet gorgeous mother of the bride dress.

"You look beautiful. You didn't need something with extra shoulder pads," I teased.

"She does look wonderful. It seems like just yesterday our kids were just meeting on the playground," he said with a sigh, his hand over his heart.

He looked ready to cry, but the mother of the bride just waved me off and handed him a handkerchief.

"I was supposed to be the blubbering mess. Not you."

"I can't help it. Our kids are finally tying the knot."

"I'm so happy for all of you. Now I'm going to go see Tracy and her attendants."

"I'll be in there soon. Just giving her a break so that way she can talk about things that I don't need to hear about." She winked as she said it, and the father of the groom laughed, and I shook my head, knowing that this was a good family, and they all seemed to get along. That's at least counted as a win in my book.

I made my way up to the bride's room and knocked slightly as I walked in.

"Good morning."

"Oh, you're here. I'm so glad that we did an early afternoon wedding, rather than a late evening one with the sunset. I'm just so happy." She began to clap as she stood in a silk robe, with her underpinnings all ready to go.

"I can't wait to see you in your gown. We're getting up to that time."

"I know. We all just had brunch, and now we're having a glass of champagne and calling it a mimosa with a spritz of orange juice."

"Would you like a glass?" the maid of honor asked, and I shook my head.

"A little too early for me if you want me to stay on track of everything else. But I promise I will have one at the reception."

"That sounds like a deal. Everything is so lovely, Alexis. Thank you for helping me plan my dream wedding." Tracy reached out and gripped my hands, tears filling her gaze, and I smiled right back.

"Thank you for being a beautiful and understanding bride."

"She has been obnoxiously chipper and happy and agreeable," the maid of honor said with a grin.

"I'm trying not to be a bridezilla. I assume I'll be that way when I'm pregnant. You know, the one with all the hormones and cravings. So I'm trying to be good here."

"You're not doing too badly," I teased.

"Seriously, with the way that Luke and Tracy look at each other, it's nauseating. But in the best ways."

"They are pretty sweet together."

"Just as sweet as you and a certain owner of this establishment," Tracy teased, fluttering her eyelashes.

I froze, just an instant, but I did my best to keep the smile on my face.

"Let's get you in that dress," I deflected, and all the girls started to giggle, waving their hands in the air.

"We saw the way you and Eli looked at each other. It's so sweet. The wedding planner in love." Tracy held her hands up to her chest and sighed, and ice slid over me.

I had been in love before, and it had broken me. What would happen when that love that I didn't feel for Eli changed? I would have nowhere else to go. I'd lose this new family I had made just when it was starting to sink in. I had to do better. I had to make sure that I wouldn't break again. That Eli wouldn't get hurt either.

The maid of honor must have seen the panic in my gaze because she pulled Tracy away, gave me an apologetic look, and I put on my most professional face again.

We got Tracy in her gown, and everything else started from there.

Photos, smiles, and the most beautiful bride I had ever seen.

Everybody was where they needed to be, and each of the Wilder brothers had shown up, even if they were behind the scenes, helping where they could.

Even Evan and Elijah had come with the winery staff to ensure that the Wilder Wines used at the wedding were top-notch.

I noticed that Kendall and Evan stood on opposite ends of the room no matter where they were, and I knew it was conscious because they always knew where the other one was.

Just like I always knew where Eli was.

I sighed and then went back to work.

The ceremony continued, with only a few little issues that the bride and groom would never know about. I was always there, doing four things at once, but it was my favorite job. I loved this. I loved seeing the happiness on their faces, even as fear began to slide onto mine as Tracy's words echoed through my head over and over again.

Once the bride and groom were on the dance floor, I let out a breath and I made my way through my next checklist, ensuring that everything was ready to go when the bride and groom left for their honeymoon. Most of the rest of the family and wedding attendants would stay at the inn one more night, but the bride and groom had a plane to catch for the red-eye.

I walked by Kendall, who grinned at me and then went back to her conversation with LJ. I nearly blinked at that, realizing that LJ Dodge was here as a guest of the groom, but I figured I might like that guy. Yes, his brother and his father were assholes, but LJ seemed nice. With the way that he was leaning into Kendall, my friend might as well. I would have to ask, but after I tried to keep Evan from punching the man for daring to talk to his ex-wife. Oh, that was going to get complicated.

I moved around the farmhouse, down the stone path so I could check on a few back-end things, and ran smack into a hard chest. I looked up, and the blood drained from my face.

"Clint? What are you doing here?"

He looked down at me, tilted his head, and gripped my arm.

"I told you. We need to talk."

Chapter Fourteen

Eli

I turned the corner, a smile playing on my face since I was on my way to find Alexis. Today was a damn good day. I had started my morning with a gorgeous woman in my arms, had a delicious breakfast that had made Alexis moan and pinken all over. And now this event was going off so well we already had consults, according to Elliot, about upcoming events, Not just weddings. But retirement parties, family reunions, and just full-fledged vacations as a group where they wanted our property.

I was so relieved.

I couldn't let anyone know how relieved, though, because then they would know I had been worried. But I had been. So damn worried that I had brought us all into this mistake.

But now, there was even another wine club, one that Elijah had been trying to woo for the year we had been open to the public, coming to us. They wanted our wines. And that meant we were one step closer to having things make sense.

I was so fucking thrilled because I wasn't sure what we were going to do if this hadn't worked out as well as it had.

I had thought for so long that I had been throwing my family into this mess, but maybe, just maybe, it could work. It didn't all blow up after this. But in order for that to settle inside me, I needed to see Alexis. No matter what happened, I needed to see her. Thank her.

I finished turning that corner, and my heart leapt into my throat, rage slamming into me. My feet hit the stone walkway at a rapid staccato, and I pulled a guy off Alexis.

The damn man had had his hands on her. Had dug his fingers into her arm and had pushed her against the side of the building. I ground my teeth together and pulled the man off of her, growling like a bear protecting its territory.

"Get your fucking hands off her."

The other man spat at me. "Who the hell do you think you are? You don't get to just touch me like that. What are you, some form of blue-collar asshole who thinks he can just rough up anybody that he wants to?"

I stood in the man's face. "That's rich, since your hands were on Alexis just now."

He sneered. "We were having a conversation. You don't know what you're talking about."

"I saw your hands on her. So you can get the fuck off my property right now."

The other man narrowed his gaze as his lips twitched. "Oh, the famous Wilder brother. The roughneck who doesn't know what he's doing and thinks he can just show up in this town and have people eat out of the palm of his hand? You don't fit in, and you never will."

I blinked at the other man, trying to understand what the fuck his problem was.

Alexis pushed past me. "Clint, go home. Eli, just stop."

I looked at her, and then at the other man, and realized that this was her ex-husband. The man who had hurt her and now had physically hurt her. No, I wasn't just going to stop. "First off, I don't even think you know what the fuck a roughneck is. Second, we're outside of San Antonio, the seventh-largest city in the country. This is not a small town, as much as you think it is. So you back the fuck off. Third. And probably this should have been first. If you ever come near this property again, or Alexis, me pulling you away from is going to be the least of your troubles."

"Eli," Alexis snapped beside me.

I moved so I was in front of her, blocking her from Clint's view. The other man's gaze narrowed as he noticed the action, and then he smirked again. "I see, fucking the boss. That's nice."

Alexis moved past me. "Go to hell, Clint. Eli, stop. I'm fine. Everything's fine."

"It's not fine. Get off the property, Clint." My voice was a low growl.

"Make me."

I rolled my shoulders back but only stopped moving forward when Alexis put her hand on my arm.

"Please stop. This is embarrassing."

I looked at her, at the fact that we were gaining somewhat of a crowd, and cursed under my breath. "Go," I growled softly to the other man. "Before I lose my temper."

"Fuck you."

Because I had turned my attention to Alexis, I didn't see the fist coming until it was too late. Clint's fist slammed into my jaw, but he was smaller than me, and I barely staggered back. Oh, the pain shocked me, and I rubbed at the sting and narrowed my eyes.

"Did you really just hit me?" I asked, narrowing my gaze.

"Fuck you." Clint tried again, but this time I ducked the swinging arm and took him out by the legs. It was a quick move, one that Evan had taught me years ago, and Clint was down on the ground, the breath knocked out of him.

"What the fuck, man?" I asked, shaking my head. "Really? That's what you're doing. You're banned from the property. You come here again? I'm calling the cops." I let out a breath. "Unless you want me to call the cops right now for assaulting Alexis and me."

"Eli. Just let it alone." I could hear the anger and mortification in her voice, but I couldn't focus on her. I couldn't look at her just then because I needed to ensure that this man didn't do something that would cause an issue. If I looked at Alexis at that moment, I wasn't sure what I would do. Carry her off like a caveman? Or hold her close and never let go?

"We got a problem here?" Evan asked as he came forward, the rest of my brothers showing up along with Amos.

"Oh, great. This is just great," Alexis mumbled under her breath.

I narrowed my eyes at the asshole on the ground. "Not a problem. We came to make sure this guy's never back on our property."

"We can make that happen," East growled before he pulled Clint up by his shoulders and practically dragged him away.

Evan was right by his side, helping, while Elijah led out of breath and followed.

Elliot and Everett stood behind, staring at us before they cleared their throats. "We'll go make sure everybody's okay out there."

"No, that's my job," Alexis said as she pushed forward.

"Alexis."

She whirled on me, her shoulders shaking. "I asked you to stop. I asked you to stop, and you didn't."

"He had his hands on you."

Out of the corner of my eye, I saw the rest of my family fade into the background, moving away to give us privacy. Something switched inside me, and I didn't know what the hell was going on.

"Alexis." Anger and resentment began to whirl within me, but all I could do was hold myself back to make sure I didn't drag Alexis away to ensure she was unharmed.

"Don't. I'm so embarrassed, Eli. You understand that?"

I blinked, shocked. "What do you have to be embarrassed about?"

She threw her hands in the air. "My ex-husband was here, and he hit you." Her hand went up to my face and then let it fall, and she blinked quickly. "He *hit* you. And you just threw him on the ground like it was nothing. You should have just stopped. And let me handle it."

"Let you handle it? He had you pressed up against the wall. How was that you handling it?"

Her hands were shaking, but I could see the anger and fear in her eyes. "I was going to handle it. And you came up right when he surprised me. I can take care of myself, Eli. Maybe I didn't do a good enough job about it before, but I can do it. I'm good on my own."

And right then, I knew we weren't just talking about what just happened. Now we were going to finish what had made her act so weird this morning leaving my place.

"Alexis. You don't have to handle everything on your own."

"Says the man who has to do everything on his own

here. Who built an entire business so he could be with his family and still take care of everybody."

I narrowed my eyes, but I couldn't let her walk away like this. I knew she was hurting and scared, so I would take anything she gave. I had to. Because she never lashed out and needed me. Or so I told myself. "Ouch. But that has nothing to do with what just happened here."

"It has everything to do with it. People just watched that. We created a scene at somebody else's wedding, and I have to hope to hell that the bride and groom don't hear about this. This is the perfect wedding for them, and I refuse to ruin it. I refuse to let my past ruin anything else."

"This wasn't you."

"Wasn't it? No, don't answer that. I have to go."

"Let me walk with you." Anxiety ramped up, and I pushed it down.

She whirled on me, anger in her gaze. "No. I can handle this. And you know what? Maybe this is a sign."

"What's a sign?" I asked, my heart racing.

"Like this is just complicated. Way too complicated. You're my boss. And here you are, pushing down my ex-husband without even breathing heavily. You didn't even move when he hit you."

"It was a weak-ass punch."

"And that's my ex-husband. The man that I married. The man with a weak-ass punch makes a scene, and I'm still there. But you didn't listen to me, Eli. I said I can handle it, and you didn't let me."

"Because you didn't have to."

"And you didn't let me," she repeated. "I can't do this. I need to focus on this wedding and the ones coming up. I told you this was a mistake, I shouldn't have said yes before."

"Don't do this."

"I have to. It's over, Eli. It's just better if it's over now before it gets too complicated and more feelings get involved. I'm sorry. I'll see you at our next meeting, but I just need to think." And then she shifted in her heels, pushed her shoulders back, and I knew she had her face on that was a shield of the wedding planner. She wasn't the woman that was just pressed against the wall and surprised anymore.

No, she wore her armor like a shield and left me in the dust. And it broke me.

Everett slid out of the darkness, worry on his face.

I let out a breath. "So I guess you saw all of that?" I asked dryly.

"Yeah. And you should have let Alexis handle it."

I whirled on him. "Are you fucking kidding me?

You're just going to let a woman handle that on her own? When some man has his hands on her?"

My brother held up his own hands in surrender. "I'm not saying it would be easy, but Alexis is strong. And if she's saying she needed to handle something on her own, then you should have let her."

"Fuck that. He was hurting her."

"And you pulled him off of her, and then you should have listened to what she wanted. Instead of creating a scene."

"Clint is the one who created the scene," I growled, annoyed.

"True. But maybe things would've worked differently if Alexis could've been able to handle it."

"You weren't here for all of it. You don't fucking know."

"Then I don't. And I'm wrong. But Alexis just walked away from you. Angry, hurt, and it sounds like it's over. So you better fucking fix it. Because I like her. She's good for you. Just make sure you're good for her."

Stunned, I watched my brother walk away, and I had to wonder what the fuck had just happened. How the hell had this become my fault? I thought I was helping.

And then I realized she *left* me. It was over.

And I couldn't do a damn thing about it.

Chapter Fifteen

Alexis

My heart hurt, and my head wasn't faring much better. Not when I sat in my little cabin, my home, all thanks to the Wilder brothers, and felt as if nothing would be okay again.

After the incident with Clint and Eli, I'd walked back into the wedding area and smiled, pretending that everything was just fine.

The bride and groom left for their honeymoon without a hitch, and nobody that was part of the wedding party or family found out what happened.

Only a few people from the wine club had seen the

241

incident. And they had ended up being on the sides of the guys, from what I could tell. In other words, I had been the one who had overreacted.

And yet, should I have stayed back? I couldn't have. Things had gotten so serious so quickly, and then Eli had walked up to see Clint.

I was resolute in the fact that I could have handled it on my own. Clint had never once touched me like that, but I could have handled it.

But Eli hadn't given me the opportunity to do so.

Instead, he had fought for me.

I was so embarrassed. Maybe that's why I pushed him away. Because the consequences of my own actions were coming back to me constantly, and I didn't want Eli to be one of those consequences.

I looked down at my planners, my tablet, and the scheduling that I had to do, and I was grateful I had scheduled off time today just to recuperate from the first wedding for me here. I didn't have to meet with any other brides or grooms or other people today. All I had to do was answer a few phone calls, but even then I was working towards trying to take today off as much as possible, so I was ready and not burned out.

Yet, I hadn't slept the night before. Not when all I could do was think about how Eli had taken out Clint so easily.

I could barely breathe.

I didn't know if what I had done was the right choice or if I was already regretting it.

I just couldn't make that decision, or even think at all, and that meant that maybe I had done the right thing by doing the hard thing.

Someone knocked at my door, and my stomach clenched. Did I want it to be Eli? Or did I want it never to be him again so I wouldn't have to face him?

But I wasn't a chicken. I wasn't a coward. So I would see exactly who it was and deal with the consequences.

I looked through the peephole and blinked, opening the door, confusion settling over my face.

"Kendall? Maddie? What are you guys doing here?"

"We're here because you didn't tell us what happened last night. We had to hear it from Evan of all people." Kendall stomped past me, a tray of food in her arms, while Maddie held two bottles of wine.

"It's a little early for wine, don't you think?" I asked, wondering why those were the words that came out of my mouth.

Maddie shook her head. "First, shut your face. It's never too early for wine when you work on a winery. And these are the new rosés that we've been trying, and I'm happy with them. But I need you to be happy with them, so think about it as work. We'll be taking notes."

Kendall sighed. "And I brought cheese. Lots of cheese. And vegetables and meat and bread so that way you actually eat something. Because with all that happened last night—and you didn't tell us about any of it—nor have you left your house today, you need to eat. Because, clearly, you're not taking care of yourself."

I looked between these two women who had somehow become my close friends in such a short period of time and promptly burst into tears.

"Okay, sit down and tell us what happened. We've got you." Maddie put her arm around my shoulder, and I let out of shaking breath, annoyed with myself.

"Why am I crying? I'm fine. I'm really fine."

"Yes, you are fine. But it's okay that you're stressing out right now. This is a very stressful time."

I snorted. I couldn't help it. "What's wrong with me?"

"You're having a tough day. It's okay."

"What did that asshole do to you?"

"Are we talking about Clint? Or Eli?" Maddie asked, and I winced.

"How much do you know?"

"Clearly not enough," Maddie said as she tapped my hand.

"Now, talk to us. We're here for you. I promise."

"It's just so embarrassing."

"It shouldn't be embarrassing. Nothing that you say is going to make us think any worse of you. You just need to tell us what's going on."

I looked at these two women, at everything that had changed in the past few months, and swallowed hard, and finally told them everything.

About Clint, about the money.

About the divorce and my worries. Everything.

And they sat there, asked a few questions, but didn't seem to judge me.

At least not right away.

But I was judging myself.

"That asshole. I'm glad that Eli stood up for you. But he shouldn't have had to."

I shook my head. "I just feel so stupid."

"You shouldn't. It is not your fault that he did this."

"But he only was here because of me, because he wants something. What am I supposed to do with that?"

Kendall leaned forward. "Do not let it be your problem." I blinked, but Kendall just shrugged. "All of this is on Clint. All of it. You didn't ask him to come here. You didn't ask him to be a complete fuck face who is trying to ruin everything. And yes, it's annoying when the Wilder brothers think that they can do whatever they want to try to protect you, but remember this, they came to help you. Eli protected you when he was worried you couldn't do it yourself."

"I could protect myself," I growled, even though it was halfhearted at best.

Kendall raised a hand. "You know what, you're right. I'm sorry, I was wrong for saying that. But the thing is, the Wilder brothers are wired a certain way."

"An 'egotistical man' sort of way?" I grumbled, but surprisingly, Kendall shook her head.

"They will let you fight your battles. They will hold your coat when you do. But they will also protect those they care about when nobody else will. I know that you wanted to stand up for yourself, and you wanted to be the one to protect yourself, and maybe you could have. But in the end, Clint had you against the wall, and Eli was the one who did something."

"It's just so embarrassing."

"I know it is. But that's not on you. None of this was on you."

"Are you sure? Because it feels like it was."

"It's not. It can't be. Eli isn't going to blame you for what happened. It's not on him or you to fix it completely."

"I just feel so stupid."

"Don't. I know that's silly to say, just an easy way

out. But don't feel stupid. The Wilder brothers want to protect their own."

"But I'm not Eli's."

She gave me a sad smile. "You're as close as. I see the way you two are around each other. It's okay to want it. To enjoy the way that he is with you."

My lips tugged into a smile. "Really? That's what you're going with?"

She shrugged, pushed her hair back. "It's the truth. It may not sound like the best thing, but it's the truth."

"I just don't know." That was the problem. I didn't know if I could let myself want more. Not after all the things Clint had done.

"And you ended things last night?" Maddie asked, her voice soft.

I swallowed hard. "I think so? I told him I wanted things to be over, that it was too much. That working together, living near one another, and dating was just too much. Maybe it is. Clint came here during my work, during a wedding, and could've ruined it."

"But he didn't. And yes, Eli took out that man quickly, but he did it after Clint threw the first punch."

"Is it more that you're worried about Eli acting as Clint did?" Maddie asked, and I shook my head and then shrugged.

"I don't know. Maybe? It's just complicated." My

247

heart hurt, and I didn't know what to do—something so unlike me it worried me.

"Of course, it's complicated. It's a relationship. You care about him."

I winced at Maddie's words. "I do care. And that's scary."

"It's supposed to be scary," Kendall whispered. "Because you don't know when you're going to fall, and suddenly you're there, and there's no safety net. We have nowhere to run or to hide because it's open, and you can't change things."

She swallowed hard, and Maddie and I gave her a moment to compose herself.

"I don't know what I want. Everything is still so new that I should be able to have time to just think. To enjoy the moments, but with the added complications of working together, and being so close, and never having an escape, and even being surrounded by all of his family and people that just know him, it makes things difficult."

"It is. But all relationships are difficult in some ways." Maddie winced. "Why do you think I'm so nervous around Elijah?"

"And are you ever going to do anything about that?" I asked, interested.

The other woman shook her head. "No. But things are different for me than they are for you."

"It sure doesn't feel like it right now."

"The Wilders make bad decisions. They're good at that. But then when they make the right ones, they tend to make up for it." I looked at Kendall, surprised at her words. "Don't look at me like that."

"I can't help it. It's odd to hear those words coming out of your mouth."

She shrugged. "Wilder's grovel like no other. And sometimes you can accept it. Sometimes you can't. All I'm saying is if Eli's brothers get through to him like we're trying to get through to you, he might actually apologize."

"And the question is, what are you going to do about it?"

I looked at both of them, swallowed hard, but I didn't have answers. Instead, I tasted the wine, took notes, loved the rosé, ate what Kendall told me to. And didn't talk about the Wilder's, or work, for another thirty minutes. I just let myself be for that time.

And when they left, since all of us did have work on our plates, I still didn't know what I was going to say when and if Eli showed up.

Of course, I didn't have long to think because someone knocked on the door again, and when I looked to see the hulking shadow out there, I was just forever grateful it wasn't Clint.

Instead, Eli stood there, his hands in his pockets, a frown on his face.

"Hey," I said as I opened the door.

"I wasn't sure you were even going to open that. Not that I would have blamed you with how I acted last night."

Was this the Wilder Grovel? Why did I feel like a lech standing here in front of him?

"Eli. I'm sorry."

His eyes widened. "Why are you apologizing?"

"Because I shouldn't have pushed you away as I did. I was just so embarrassed, and I guess there is no coming back from that."

He shook his head. "Of course, there's coming back from that. I just felt terrible that I didn't even let you settle down with whatever had happened, and I know you've wanted to say a few things, and we haven't had the chance, and so here I am, hoping you'll forgive me and understand that I know I'm an asshole, but I didn't mean to be one this time."

I shook my head, winced. "Eli. Things are just so complicated with us."

"They are, but aren't they for most people?"

"Maybe. Or maybe it shouldn't have to be."

"I'm here to grovel, to apologize, and to say I'm a crock of shit."

I couldn't help it. I burst out laughing, shaking my head. "Really? That's what you're going with."

"Relationships are hard. Sometimes they're harder than others, and we all have baggage. Hell, you're living on a resort with my baggage. It is surrounded by you. It's on the goddamn letterhead."

My lips threatened to turn up into a smile. "Eli."

"We all have baggage. And Clint might be part of yours, but you're not solely responsible for who he is or the choices he makes."

"He came here. He hurt you."

Finally, I let myself reach up and touch his bruised chin. He didn't wince, didn't move back. Instead, he leaned into the touch, and tears threatened again.

"Alexis."

"He hurt you."

"Would I see bruises on your arms if I were to take that sweater of yours off?"

"Maybe." I winced, and his eyes went cloudy. "He hurt you, too."

"I should've called the cops."

"And that would have just been another scene."

"I still don't like it. The fact that he was here."

"And I don't even know what he wanted. Money?

251

Power? Me? Who knows. I don't understand him, but you kicked him off the property, and the wedding seemed to have still gone off well, and so maybe I overreacted."

He shook his head, leaned forward to cup my face as my hands fell. "I'm the one who's sorry. You asked me to stop. To move out of the way so you can handle it, and I didn't because I was angry. Because I thought I could handle it. But I should've let you do it. I'm going to try to do better. But know I will still make mistakes. I'm not the greatest at it. But I will try."

I shook my head and leaned into him, letting his arms fall, so they wrapped around me. "I'm not good at this. As is evidenced by my divorce."

"My evidence is that I don't even have a marriage or a divorce to lean back on. So how's that for relationship experience?"

"I'm scared, Eli. I wasn't expecting you."

He looked down at me then and then brushed his lips on mine. "I wasn't expecting you either."

"So, I guess we should learn how to do better."

In answer, I tugged on his shirt, and he came inside, closing the door behind him.

His eyes widened marginally and I laughed, letting him slowly run his hands down me.

"I want you," he growled.

"Good. Because I want you too." I paused, looked up at him. "The bruises are shallow, fading already. I don't want you to get angry."

"You can't tell me what to feel, but I promise I won't go find him and beat him up. How's that?"

I grinned, reached up, and cupped his bruised cheek again. "Okay. I promise the same."

He kissed me again, and I was lost.

He moved me towards my love seat, gently pressing me against the back of it. When he pulled up my sweater, his eyes widened, and I blushed.

"I didn't feel like putting on a bra today."

He cleared his throat, his cheeks going red as his gaze went to my naked breasts.

"Thank God."

He leaned down and gently sucked one nipple into his mouth, and then the other.

I moaned, pressing my body into his as he sucked on my breasts, hard, so hard in fact, the slight pain nearly sent me over the edge. He cupped my free breast, plucking at my nipple, gently at first, and then harder. I pressed my thighs together, my body quaking, as he slowly slid his hands down the front of my leggings.

"No panties either. I like this."

"It was my lazy day."

He tugged on my hair slightly, pulling my head back

so that he could latch on my mouth. I groaned, letting out a shocked gasp when his hand went over my pussy.

"There's going to be nothing lazy about what I do to you now."

"Whatever you say, Eli."

And then his fingers were inside me, and I was shaking, rocking my hips over his hands. He fucked me, with his fingers, in and out, both of us shaking, kissing at one another. He kissed my lips, then bit down on my shoulder, using his free hand to play with my breasts. And then when he looked up, and my hips were rocking, he grinned.

"That's it, Alexis. Fuck my hand. Know it's my hand inside you. I'm the one that is touching you, bringing you to orgasm. Now, help me fuck you."

With his words, I came, my pussy clamping around his fingers. He groaned, and when I finally fell down into the abyss, he slid his hands from beneath my leggings and then sucked his fingers, his gaze on me.

I clamped my thighs together, shaking at the sight. And when he put his wet fingers along my lips, I opened my mouth, letting him slide his fingers inside my mouth, over my tongue. I sucked and licked myself off of his skin, blushing, and then his mouth was on mine, a crushing and bruising kiss. When he stripped my leggings down, I moaned and let out a shocked gasp as I found myself bent over the couch, my ass in the air, and his cock pressed against me. I hadn't even realized he had begun to strip down, but then my hair was tangled in his fist, my toes were barely touching the ground, and he was ramming into me, hard and fast and wet and hot.

I clutched the edge of the couch, bringing myself up so I could arch into him, taking him in deeper. And he groaned, both of us shaking with need. And when I could feel myself nearing completion, I steadied myself on one hand and gripped my breast, squeezing my nipple. I came again, this time around his cock, and when he groaned, bit down on my neck again, I shook, my whole body flushed and red and hot, and I could barely breathe or think or do anything.

Then he was out of me again, and I was twisting, my ass on the edge of the couch as my thighs were splayed wide, my hips rocking as he pumped into me again, this time facing me, and I gripped his shoulders, my nails digging into his skin for dear life. He grinned, fucking me hard, as I slammed right back into him. And then he was coming, I was following him, and it was sweaty and hot and sticky and meant everything.

This wasn't a grovel or an apology. No, this was us finally coming together.

This had nothing to do with who I had been or who

I even wanted to be. This was who we were in the moment. This was all I needed.

And as I fell onto him, needing him.

I was afraid that I had fallen.

And I wasn't ready.

But there was no resisting a Wilder. Even when you tried.

Chapter Sixteen

Alexis

Another wedding was in the books. My feet hurt, and my head hurt, but the happy couple were in the honeymoon suites and would be leaving the next day for their honeymoon. Colin and Adam had wanted a classic farm wedding, and we had given it to them.

The looks on their faces when they had said 'I do' meant the world to me. Because my job was to ensure that they only had to worry about getting to that altar and professing their love and promises to one another. Everything else was frosting on that cake, frosting that took months to make and get just right, but that was my specialty.

And they smiled, and thanked me, and had even hugged Eli and Everett.

That had made me smile, the looks of surprise and mortification when the Wilder brothers had gotten their big hugs, mostly because the Wilders did their best to hide from everyone else so that way no one knew who they were. But, there was no hiding a Wilder. They were big, sexy as hell, and were always there to help out. You couldn't hide that.

So now I sat in Eli's place, on his couch, and rested my feet on the coffee table.

I let out a small groan when someone touched my foot, and I opened one eye to see Eli sitting on the coffee table, putting my feet on his lap and rubbing the balls of my feet.

The sheer pleasure of it nearly made me cum right there, and from the moan escaping my mouth, Eli knew exactly what I was thinking.

"Why do you wear those shoes if they're going to do that to your feet?" he asked, his voice low.

I smiled up at him. "Because of the way that you look at my ass when I'm wearing those shoes."

He paused and then grinned, as if picturing my ass.

"I guess you're right. You do look sexy as hell. Plus, I've seen you wear those shoes and nothing but those shoes right before they dug into my back."

I snorted, shaking my head.

"You're ridiculous."

"Yeah, I am. But I'm me. I can't help it."

"True. The wedding went off well, though. They seemed happy."

"They were happy. And I'd like to think that we had something to do with it, but maybe it was just them."

I looked up at him, and he just shook his head, his lips forming a smile before he sighed and leaned back on the table.

"I still think it's odd that this is my job now."

I just smiled. "I think it's odd that this is your job now, too, but you're good at it."

He blinked, and I just shook my head.

"It's true. You do your best to focus on everybody and make sure that they're ready to go. Make sure that they have everything that they need."

"I don't know. Sometimes it feels like I'm just treading water, making sure that people are getting what they need, but I'm not exactly sure that I made the right decision when it came to my brothers."

I sat up, taking my foot back from him and setting it on the floor. I studied his face, the worry lines etched on his skin, and shook my head. "Eli. There's nothing more that you could be doing. You made sure that they all had somewhere to go after finding their new lives. You've done amazing."

"It doesn't always feel like that."

"Well, it should. Your brothers are happy, or at least finding it." He raised a brow at that, and I shrugged. "Finding it is a better description, but it's their jobs that are letting them have that steady place to come back to when they're figuring everything else out. And you're the one who came up with this idea to make it happen."

"Sometimes I feel like my following in Roy's footsteps could have been either the worst decision I ever made, or the best."

"I don't think you're giving yourself enough credit."

He smiled at me then, shaking his head.

"Sometimes I think I'm giving myself just the right amount."

"You're a good big brother, and they're adults. They're making their own choices."

"Well, I guess a good choice that I made was bringing you on."

I rolled my eyes. "I supposed me saying yes, or even applying for this job, was a good choice."

He grinned then and leaned forward, brushing his lips on mine. Gooseflesh pebbled over my skin, and I swallowed hard, sliding my hands down his chest.

"You taste like champagne," he whispered.

I blushed. "I had a single glass at the end of the night to celebrate."

"I'm sure I can get some more because I want to taste it on your skin."

I groaned, sliding deeper into the couch when someone knocked on the front door.

I blinked up at Eli, who frowned, and made his way to the front door. My phone buzzed at that moment, and I looked down to see texts from an unknown number.

Unknown: *I told you we need to talk. Tell your brute to leave off.*

I sighed, embarrassment crawling over me, and blocked the number.

I was going to have to change my phone number at this point, but since I also needed a public work number, he would always be able to find it because of the inherent nature of my job.

I shook my head as Eli's voice reached me.

"Eliza? What are you doing here? Did I know you were coming? And here, give me the baby."

"I'm so sorry. I thought you knew. I told Evan."

A woman with dark hair and a bright smile walked in, after handing over a small bundle to Eli. A man with dark hair, blue eyes, and who looked to be about the same size as Eli walked in behind the woman who Eli had called Eliza.

In other words, his sister.

Who was now walking into the living room and seeing me in a very odd state of near-undress after a long day.

If I could hide underneath this couch right then, I would.

"Oh. You have company." Eliza blinked. "And you're Alexis. Oh, my God. It's so great to meet you. It's hard to get any details out of Eli, but thankfully, he has brothers who tell me everything."

I swallowed hard, nearly choking, as I stood up and remembered that I was barefoot and nearly tripped over my shoes. "Hi," I whispered. "And what did they tell you? No, I don't want to know."

"All good things, I promise. Oh, it's so good to finally meet you in person." Eliza hugged me tightly, and instinctively I hugged her right back, and right then and there, there was another click. Similar to what had happened with Eli and me; it felt like I had known this woman my entire life.

What was it about the Wilder siblings?

"Evan knew you were coming here?"

"He did. We were coming for the weekend because

I have a consult out here, and we're staying in one of the cabins. It took a while to get out here, though, because our plane was delayed. Evan said we should meet you here. And, apparently, he hasn't told you anything."

The man speaking looked over me and smiled. "I'm Beckett Montgomery. This is Lexington. Nice to meet you."

"I'm Alexis, and I am in the way."

"You're not in the way, so don't you dare think that you can go right now," Eliza said with a grin. "I can't wait to get to know you."

"And you can get to know me tomorrow. When I haven't just finished with a wedding, and I look like this."

"You look amazing. I don't know what you're worried about. I have just been traveling with a baby for the first time on a plane. Talk to me after that."

She winked as she said it, and she wrapped her arms around my shoulders.

"So, you're the mysterious guest that Evan said was coming for Cabin A."

"And you didn't think to ask?" Eliza asked, grinning.

"I've been a little preoccupied," he grumbled, and I blushed harder.

"I should really go."

"No, no," Eli said as he shook his head and ran his hands through his hair. "Alexis, this is my baby sister Eliza, and her husband, Beckett. The baby is Lexington. My favorite baby ever. Y'all, this is Alexis. The Wilder wedding planner and the woman that I'm seeing. Which you all know. Now, I don't know why Evan said to come up here other than to probably just to get my goats, but let me take you to the cabin."

"I can find it." Eliza shook her head, looking contrite. "You've just finished with a wedding. Take your time. Stay here. We're the ones intruding."

The baby started patting Beckett's chest. He looked down at it. And right then, my ovaries exploded.

Yes, I had fallen in love with Eli Wilder.

A man, a big man, holding a tiny baby to his chest as that baby tried to reach his beard. That's what did it. That's what made me fall.

And from the knowing look on Eliza's face, Eli's baby sister knew exactly what had just happened.

Well, damn it.

"Seriously, enjoy your time, go yell at Evan for trying to be sneaky and apparently succeeding, and I will see you tomorrow."

"You don't have to go," Eli whispered as he leaned down.

Knowing everyone was looking, including baby

Lexington, I went up to my tiptoes and kissed him softly. Everybody already knew what we were doing. It wasn't like I should hide kissing him.

He looked surprised for a moment, but that just warmed me. Because he wasn't sure how I was going to react, and frankly, I hadn't been either.

"I'm going to go, so that way you can spend time with your family, and tomorrow I will see all of you when I look presentable and not like a hot mess."

I looked down at the baby in Eli's arms. "It's nice to meet you, Lexington."

The baby reached out and patted my cheek, and I leaned into his little pudgy hands.

"You're seriously adorable."

"He's a menace. But he's our menace," Eliza whispered. "We're sorry for kicking you out."

"I'm not being kicked out. I am calmly walking home so I can take a shower after a very long day. I will see you tomorrow. I promise."

I said my goodbyes, knowing I was leaving a bit awkwardly, but I needed a moment. I hadn't expected to meet Eli's sister the way I did, or the fact that everyone now seemed to know much more about my personal business than I was expecting. Not that I blamed them because Maddie and Kendall knew a lot about my thoughts with Eli, but I was still coming to terms with that.

I was in love with Eli Wilder.

How the hell had that happened?

One minute I was trying to find my new way, my new life, a newly divorced woman who was starting from the ground up.

The next, I was in love with a man who was holding a baby and who was almost a father-figure to Eliza and the rest of their siblings.

My life wasn't supposed to be this complicated, and yet, did I want anything to change? Did I want to go back to the way things were?

It scared me because I wasn't sure what my answer should be.

Because I knew my answer was that I loved Eli.

And I loved the way that our life was turning out. Even if it was changing on a dime, and we're still settling into it.

Panic began to creep in, but I did my best to ignore it.

Because I would figure this out, I always did.

I moved my way down the path, noting that the rest of the guests were all tucked into their rooms, and while the floodlights were on so that way I was never in the dark, I was glad that I was heading home. I just wanted to go to bed and wake up so I could be fresh-faced when I saw Eliza and the rest of them again.

I turned the corner, and something sharp slammed into the back of my head. I fell, my knees digging into the tile, and there was pain, a grumble, and then nothing.

Chapter Seventeen

Eli

"We didn't mean to kick her out," Eliza said as she bit her lip. I hugged baby Lexington closer and frowned. "It's okay. We're still taking things slow."

"Just because you're taking things slow doesn't mean she had to run away at the sight of us." Eliza sighed as Beckett wrapped his arm around her shoulders. "It's okay, babe. She probably gets enough of the Wilder brothers as it is. Adding one more Wilder to the mix, even though she's a Montgomery now, was probably too much."

"Hey, once a Wilder, always a Wilder," I mock growled as I patted Lexington's diapered bottom.

"You say that, and yet all I hear is Montgomery." Beckett grinned, then plucked Lexington from my arms, and did the sniff test. "We're okay for now, but I have a feeling dinner's about to make its way south."

I grimaced. "I don't understand how you guys are so okay with talking about bodily functions like that."

"You were in the military and have how many brothers? I think you'd be just fine," Beckett added with a grin, but I still looked towards the door, wondering if I should have made Alexis stay. Or, hell, walked her to her cabin. That's what I should have done. What the hell was wrong with me?

"Come on, let's go get settled, yell at Evan, and then you can go check on her. And maybe even spend the night with her because I'm sure that's what you guys were planning here until we ruined it."

I looked down at my baby sister, then wrapped my arms around her shoulders. "I don't know what Evan was thinking, but I do like the surprise. But of course, it caught me off guard." I kissed the top of her head, and she looked up at me, grinning.

"That's what a surprise is. It's supposed to catch you off guard."

I kept frowning, though, as I thought about Alexis

and figured that yes, I would go see her after I got my sister settled. I hated that she had left like that, but Alexis liked first impressions that made sense. So meeting Eliza as she had was probably a little too much for her. But I hadn't missed the way that she had looked at me holding Lexington, the way that she had frowned for just the barest instant before she smiled and said her goodbyes. And she had kissed me in front of them, just a gentle kiss, but she had claimed me. And damn it, I would claim her too.

Because all I could do was think about that connection, that spark on that dance floor over two years ago now.

And I wanted it again.

I slid my shoes on, then followed Beckett out the door as we made our way downstairs. Evan stood in the empty hallway, and while I frowned at him, Eliza let out a gleeful sound and ran to him. She threw her arms around him but didn't throw her entire body at him like she used to. Evan seemed to realize that there was a difference too, but then his baby sister was holding him tight, and nothing else mattered. I agreed. Nothing else did matter. Not right then.

"You're here. And you're a jerk for not telling the others that we'd be here." She punched Evan in the shoulder, and I just grinned.

"See, you're the jerk."

"Teaching our kid about punching already. Now who's the bad influence?"

Eliza just rolled her eyes. "Excuse me. But the Montgomerys are way worse than the Wilders."

"It's true," Evan and I said at the same time, and we laughed.

Beckett just shook his head. "Not even a little."

"You're outnumbered here, Montgomery. Just remember that." I plucked Lexington back from Beckett's arms but then frowned as Evan took the kid from me.

"My turn," Evan said as he kissed the top of Lexington's head. The baby smiled up at him, and I just sighed, wondering how this kid already had us wrapped around his little fingers.

We made our way out the back and piled into their rental SUV to drive to the cabin that Evan had set up for them.

We could have walked, but none of us felt like dragging suitcases all around.

I'd walk back to my place, but I would stop at Alexis' first, just to make sure that she was okay and because I wanted to see her, damn it.

The rest of my brothers were all waiting at the cabin when I got there, and I frowned. "Did they all know?" I asked as I hopped out of the SUV to help Eliza.

"I just told them to meet us here, so they know now," Evan said with a grin, and I had to wonder if this was how he got his kicks these days, because the man was interesting, to say the least.

The welcome was loud, exuberant, and did good things for me. That if I hadn't forced everyone to be here in the first place, hadn't forced us to work together in such a way, we wouldn't have had this.

Other than the wedding, we rarely were together, all seven of us. Now the six of us were together every day, and Eliza visited often.

"This is because of you," Eliza whispered as she came to my side. My brothers were all passing around the baby while Beckett watched them like a hawk. Nobody was going to drop that kid, but we were standing inside underneath a ceiling fan, and since each one of us had been thrown into one as babies thanks to our equally exuberant father, it would only make sense that we were all a little worried.

"What do you mean?" I asked after a moment, her words settling in.

"You guys look happier. Maybe not all the way there yet, but a little bit better."

I frowned and shook my head. "That's them."

"They're here because of you. Because of your big idea."

"I'm just so scared that I'm fucking this up for the family."

Eliza gave me a look and sighed. "Why are you acting like this? You made a good choice."

I shook my head "I feel like I keep screwing things up."

"Is he on about this again?" Evan asked with a sigh.

"He gets this way," Elijah added.

"We're happy. Or at least we're getting there, just like our baby sister said," Elliot added.

"I would appreciate it if the baby brother would stop calling me the baby," she glared at her brother.

Elliot just shrugged and turned to me. "We love you," he said.

I blinked, wondering why the hell he was saying that. "And? You don't usually just throw that out there."

"Well, maybe you should," Eliza put in.

"Things are getting weird," East mumbled, and that earned a glare from all of us.

"I just want to make sure that we made the right decision."

"It's been two years. Yes, we made the right decision. We're happy. Get over it," Evan growled, surprising us.

"We're fine. We've got this. We're all settling down, finding our way. You don't need to worry about us this much anymore," Everett said.

"I'm always going to worry. I'm the big brother."

Beckett gave me a look. "I'm the eldest too. It comes with the job."

"I can't believe you married one of them," Elliot grumbled as he wrapped his arm around Eliza's shoulders.

"I can't either. It's like having twenty big brothers all the time between his family and ours, but look at you guys, we're together. You did a good thing, Eli. I'm proud of all of you. And, I love it here. It's gorgeous. It's like a second home."

"But we're not moving here," Beckett put in, and Eliza just rolled her eyes as the rest of my brothers put in reasons why they should move here, at least Eliza and Lexington. Beckett, they could take or leave.

I just laughed, shaking my head as Evan came to my side.

"Where's Alexis?" he asked.

I frowned. "Back at her place. She was there when Eliza and them showed up, and since it was a surprise, she didn't look as perfect as she wanted to. Even though I thought she looked perfect, not that I could actually tell her that."

"I mean, it could be worse. They could have walked in on you having sex," Evan said with a laugh.

"Well, it was nearly there," I grumbled, and Evan just laughed again.

"We're all settled here. Go get your girl. Bring her over here, or stay there. Don't make the same mistakes I did."

I froze since Evan rarely ever said anything about Kendall, but then my brother walked away, plucking the baby up and spinning him around.

I shook my head, said my goodbyes, and made my way to go get Alexis.

I loved her, damn it. I'd tried not to, but there was no holding back. Not when it came to her.

And I wanted her to hang out with my family. Fuck, I wanted her to be my family. That was probably too soon, but I wasn't good about taking things slow. Not anymore.

I made the walk around the pathway, nodding at a few guests that were sitting on their patios, enjoying a hot drink on a cool night, and knocked on Alexis' door. It was locked, and the front light was on, but I couldn't hear anything. I didn't think she would be sleeping already since it wasn't too late, but I frowned, wondering why she wasn't there.

I pulled out my phone, ready to call her, the hairs on

the back of my neck standing on end, and when I pressed her name, and heard her phone in the distance, ringing into the night air, bile slid up my throat. I ran towards the sound, seeing the phone in the grass, lighting up the area, her purse on the ground next to it.

But Alexis wasn't here.

I turned around, searching for her, but she wasn't there.

And my world fell out from beneath my feet.

Chapter Eighteen

Alexis

I tried to rub my hands together to get free of the rope and hopefully wake up from this nightmare. This couldn't be happening. Seriously, this made no sense to me at all, and yet here I was, sitting on the floor of one of the last cabins that East was renovating, surrounded by boxes of floor planks and chisels. There was sanding equipment and a saw. Everything that East was storing here out of the way of the guests and to keep it safe.

It didn't make any sense.

How could I be here?

And then I looked up at Clint, the man that I had thought I had loved, and wondered how he could have become this person.

"Don't look at me like that," Clint growled with a glare, and I blinked, swallowing hard, my hands shaking within their bounds.

"What are you thinking, Clint?"

"Shut up! How dare you? You are mine, Alexis. Mine, and you just left. You don't get to leave me, Alexis. You never did."

He moved forward, and my head fell back as his palm slapped across my face. My eyes watered, and I tried to stop shaking as he moved back and began to pace, that familiar panicked expression on his face once again.

"I just need to get through these things, and everything will be fine."

I looked at him, confused, shaking my head, trying to sound far more confident than I felt. "What things? How is it going to be fine? What are you doing, Clint?"

"I said shut up. Just shut the fuck up. It was always this way with you. I could never think when you were around." Fear ebbed within me, and I knew if I didn't find a way to calm him down and get him to let me go, it could only get worse.

He'd never hit me before, never done anything like

this. He'd been mean, had taken part of my soul, and beaten me down emotionally, but I couldn't believe this was happening.

"Clint, just let me go. This doesn't have to get any worse." I tried to keep myself as calm as possible, but I could hear the terror underneath the words.

He glared at me then, and I swallowed hard, the knife in his hand shining near the single light from the lantern on the floor. He had drawn the blinds down, but I had to hope that maybe somebody would notice the soft glow of the light.

Clint began to pace again, then set the knife on a small table, but it wasn't like I could get up and get it to try to protect myself. He would just hit me in the back of the head again as he had with the rock, and my hands were still tied behind my back.

"This wasn't how it was supposed to be. You were supposed to take me back. You were supposed to come back, the way it always should have been. Instead, you left before I could have what was mine. You were always like this. Worthless."

I shook my head. "Clint. I don't know what you want. I'm sorry."

"Of course, you know what I want. I just needed to get out of debt. How hard is it for you to understand that the money should have been ours? But no, you had to take what you thought was yours, and you took it from me. You're the reason that they're coming after me."

I blinked. "What?"

"You. Because of you, Tawny and the others are going to come for me because I made some bad bets. Some bad investments. But I was doing everything I should have. I got you the goddamn ring, didn't I? I proposed to you in the most romantic fucking way. I did everything I was supposed to do. And you didn't give me what I needed."

"Are you telling me you have a loan shark or someone after you?"

"Of course I fucking do!" he practically screamed. "Don't you understand? You knew what was happening, and yet you still left me out to dry. You dared leave me. I took everything you had. You had nothing left, and yet you still defied me. Alexis. You cannot be this stupid."

"Clint," I whispered. Fear slammed into me, but I just had to keep Clint talking. The more I did, the better chance he wouldn't do anything harsher than he already had. And that meant maybe I could get out of this. I just didn't want any of the Wilders to get involved. They had already been through so much hell before this. They didn't need anything on top of this. I didn't want Eli to get hurt. But I still wanted him to hold me.

I wanted to get out of this. I just needed to get Clint to continue to talk.

"I needed that money. And now it seems I'll have to make sure I get it another way."

Terror slammed into me. "I don't have it yet, but you can have it all, Clint. I promise. As soon as the inheritance comes to me, you can have it."

"You think that's all I want? You think that it's all money? You were *mine*, Alexis. And you just fucking walked away like you had the right."

"I'm so sorry, Clint. What can I do to make it better?" I tried to push back the rising fear, but it was a ball in my throat threatening to take over.

He began to pace some more and nearly kicked over the lantern. I sucked in a breath, knowing that if the flames hit any of the chemicals surrounding us, this whole place would go up in smoke. I swallowed hard, trying to get out of my bounds.

"Clint. Just let me go."

"I wasn't supposed to take you tonight. I was just supposed to talk to you. Or at least show you what you did wrong. But you never want to talk to me. It isn't until just now that I have you in here like a fucking idiot that suddenly you want to talk to me. I did my best not to do what you deserve. But here we are. All because of you."

My palms were sweaty, and I wanted to throw up.

"Okay. I'm here. I will get you whatever money that I have. You can have it all. Just let me go."

"It's not going to be enough. Don't you understand that? *It's not fucking enough.*"

I swallowed hard. "Okay. Then we'll find something."

"You were also always so placating. It's why our marriage didn't work out. Because you always put everyone else ahead of me, and then when you tried to think of me, you treated me like I was one of your fucking grooms that you had to pacify. Because the brides were always first."

I had a hard time keeping up, my head ached, and I knew I probably had a concussion.

"I get that. I'm sorry. I was a bad wife."

"You were. I probably wasn't the best husband either, but I can't fix that." He winked then, scaring me. My whole body went cold as he picked up the knife and walked forward.

"Clint. Please." Tears fell now in earnest, and I didn't know what I was supposed to do. How could I fight for myself when I couldn't get free? He'd taken away all my options, and now I was left here in his control.

Again.

"Shut up. I don't know what to do, Alexis. I don't

know what to do."

He picked me up so my back pressed against the wall, and then I was standing, and my eyes widened. Because he had the knife against my chin, just looking at me, the vacantness that I saw there scaring me.

"Clint," I whispered, trying not to move my jaw too much.

"I'm sorry, Alexis."

"Clint. Don't do this. You don't have to do this."

Then the door opened and Eli stood there, and I screamed, the knife scraping against my skin.

"Eli! Don't!"

"Oh, good. It's the Wilder to save you." And then everything happened at once. Eli moved forward and Clint slashed with the knife, but slipped, the angle of the blade changing. I screamed as the knife slid into my shoulder, slicing through my skin, and I fell to the ground. Blood soaked my shirt, and then Clint was moving, the knife up, and Eli was running towards him.

Yet as I hit the floor, one of the planks moved, smashing into the lantern.

And then the flames began to move over the ground, and when Clint roared, I tried to get up, ignoring the pain because this would not be how it ended.

It couldn't be.

Chapter Nineteen

Eli

Everything happened all at once, and I could barely keep up. A man came at me with a knife, the blade shining underneath the glow of firelight behind him. I cursed under my breath, realizing this was Clint, Alexis' ex-husband.

"You did this. You ruined it all."

I had no idea what the fuck he was talking about, but all I knew was that I needed to get Alexis out of there. Out of the corner of my eye, I saw her down on the ground, bleeding from her shoulder as she tried to get out of her bonds, but that's not what scared me the most. No, it was the fire slowly beginning to lick up the blinds and the wall, the canister of paint getting closer and closer.

"Jesus Christ," I mumbled under my breath.

"Fuck you!" Clint roared, and I bent down, easily dodged the knife that came at me, and punched the man in the gut. He let out an oof and fell, the knife clattering to the ground. Clint came at my knees, trying to push me into the wall, and I staggered a bit, then kicked the knife away before pulling Clint out of the cabin.

"What the fuck is going on?" Evan asked as he came forward and looked to see what I saw. A cabin nearly on fire, Alexis screaming as she stood up, blood pouring down her arm, and limping towards me.

"Get him out of here."

I turned, but Clint was not where I left him, and I saw that he had rolled to the side and was already running back into the burning cabin. He pushed past me, and I kicked at him, trying to tug him off, but he went for Alexis, hands outstretched. She pushed up her knee, connecting with the man's nuts, and Clint fell again, groaning.

"Eli. The fire," she called out

"Let's get you out of here."

Evan and Everett were there then, taking Clint out,

while Elijah, East, and Elliot were all working on the fire, one of them shouting on their phone.

My brothers were here, and we were handling it.

I leaned forward, picked up Alexis, and carried her out of the burning building. She coughed into me, and I held her close, keeping her head down.

"We're almost out."

"Was anyone else in there?" East asked, his eyes wide.

And then my brother, my fucking strong brother who looked in the face of hell every day and could do anything, went to his knees, his face pale, as he slowly began to shake. He bent over, threw up, and then Elliot was there, taking care of him. Everett stood near, pressing his hands against his eyes as he muttered to himself.

I knew why East was reacting this way, knew exactly what memories this had invoked.

My brothers were breaking. Had already broken. And that was why we'd come here. Why we'd build this home, but I couldn't help them.

East and Everett had to be okay, Elliot would take care of them.

"No one else was in there. Just get Clint out. I don't want him to die," Alexis coughed as I set her down on the ground. She staggered, and that's when I realized that she was still bleeding from the knife wound on her shoulder.

"Jesus God," I rasped as I tugged off my flannel shirt and pressed it to the wound.

"Don't do that. It's dirty. I have my bag with me."

And then Elliot was there, as Elijah sat next to East, taking care of him.

PTSD was slowly taking my brother away, and it had taken two years to bring him out of it, but the fire just then, the screaming, it wasn't going to get any better any time soon. Elliot's TBI forced him to sit down near us, but he looked better than he had already. East was being taken care of, and Elliot was by Alexis' side, helping take care of the wound on her shoulder.

"It's not too deep. You're going to be fine."

"Tell that to the screaming pain," she rasped, then looked up at me. "You're okay. You came."

"Of course I came. I've got you, Alexis."

I cupped her face and ignored the groaning from Clint as he lay curled in a ball underneath Evan. My brother had nearly hogtied him but then thought better of it as we all looked at the burning cabin and knew it would be a loss.

She breathed out heavily, her body shaking. "I'm so sorry."

I cupped her face, my own hands shaking. "It's okay. It's okay. I've got you."

"Your cabin." She tried to wipe her tears, her eyes wide, then winced at the movement.

"The fire department's on its way," Elliot whispered as he leaned closer, the fear in his gaze as alarming as mine..

Evan let out a breath. "As are the paramedics that are going to take care of you. And we're going to figure out exactly what the hell happened."

"That's my question too." I tried to stamp down my anger, but it wasn't toward Alexis. Never toward Alexis.

She leaned into me, trying to be strong, but I knew she was in pain. "I don't know what happened. I can't believe it."

"It's okay. I've got you." And I always would. No matter what happened, I would be here.

Then she sighed into me and I held her close, and I knew I could never let her go. I just had to hope she and my family could find a way to make it through this.

Whole.

Or however whole we could be.

Chapter Twenty

Alexis

I had stitches and was the proud owner of a mild concussion and would be wearing a bandage and an arm sling for a little while. Once the paramedics had come, the firemen right on their heels to take out the fire on that cabin, things were a blur.

I knew the Wilders were working together to clean up the mess that Clint had made, but there was nothing to be saved of the cabin that East had been renovating.

It was gone. If I hadn't been there, none of this would have happened.

I wasn't sure what I was supposed to do with that or how I was supposed to face them again.

But I needed to.

I sat in a hospital bed, waiting to be discharged, and people were moving quickly, with things to do, others to take care of. I felt like I was taking up space.

My parents had already called, as had my brother. They weren't going to come out here because I asked them not to, but I had a feeling there would be a family visit within the next month. Just to check on me because they cared about me. Because they were worried about me. Again.

If they had their way, I would move out to them and start my life over for what felt like the twentieth time, in Spain.

Maybe that would be the best idea. To move with my family and to leave all this behind. To leave Clint behind.

To leave Eli behind.

"I'm so glad that you're okay," Maddie said from the doorway, Kendall right beside her.

I blinked at seeing both women, startled, since I hadn't expected them to be here, but then again, I should have. They were my friends now. And they were here for me.

I wiped away tears and then they were both at my bedside, gripping my free hand.

"You look terrible, darling," Kendall whispered, then leaned down to kiss my cheek. "And we love you. Do you have enough pain meds? Do I need to go find a nurse? There's a very sexy nurse out there."

That made me laugh and then wince since it pulled at my bandage.

"His name is Jeff, and his wife is a surgeon on the top floor. She could probably dissect you quickly, and nobody would even notice that you were gone."

"I see that she has marked her territory plainly, and I respect that," Kendall said with a wink. "I am sorry for making you laugh. That didn't look like it felt nice."

"It didn't, but I'm okay. I'm okay." The tears kept falling, though, so Maddie held me close while Kendall squeezed my hand. They were both so gentle with me, and it was all I could do not to lean into them and want them to take care of everything. But I had to do this. On my own.

"The Wilders were all here, though some left to go back to take care of the property."

"How much of it was lost?" I asked, swallowing hard.

Kendall answered. "It was just that cabin. Even the land around it was saved. No trees were harmed, the path is salvageable, and because it was the one near the back, most of the guests didn't even realize there was an issue until later today. The fire trucks and paramedics went through the back loading entrance. This isn't going to be an issue for the Wilders."

I winced. "Their place almost burned down to the ground."

"One small building did, but nobody died," Maddie whispered and winced. "Which is an awful way to say that, but none of the guests were hurt. Nobody was in danger other than you, which is a very scary thing, and I never want to think about that again."

"Eli could have been hurt, though."

"And where is he? You would think you would be here?" Kendall asked, a frown on her face.

Maddie shook her head. "Eli had to deal with the authorities, and I believe Elijah and Everett joined him. East went off somewhere, Elliott with him. And Evan went back to the winery. Because the place isn't closed and we're all doing fine. It didn't hurt the resort or the winery, because I know that's what you're worried about."

"Of course, I'm worried about it."

"Don't. Breathe. I don't know where exactly you are with your relationship with Eli, because I was going to wait until later this week to corner you with cheese and wine to get the answers out of you."

That made me smile, and Kendall even chuckled.

"However, this doesn't mean you need to walk away from everything that you started with him."

"It's been a lot very quickly," I began, but Kendall was the one who spoke up, surprising me.

"We all in this room know that I will be the last person to say that happiness and marriage and futures with Wilders are easy. Because they're not, and it didn't work out for me. But I see the way you are with Eli. Don't use this as an excuse to walk away. Because excuses are so easy to come by these days, don't make the same mistakes I did."

I reached out and squeezed her hand.

"I don't know what I'm supposed to do."

"Talk with him. And heal. And talk to us. Because it was so scary, Alexis. I don't want to think about what could have happened if you hadn't gotten out when you did."

"Eli saved me."

"And you were going to find a way to save yourself, too," Kendall began. "Because it's what you do. You're so damn strong. And I'm sorry your ex-husband was an asshole."

My eyes widened. "Was?"

Kendall held up her hands. "Sorry, is. *Is* an asshole. He's alive and under arrest as far as I know."

"That's the last I heard, but you said was, and I was afraid he had died, and somehow it was my fault, and I think I'm going to throw up."

The girls held me for a minute before, finally, the nurse asked them to leave, to give me space, and I just squeezed their hands before they left, trying to find any form of positivity in what was going on.

And then there was a scuff on the floor and someone clearing their throat, and Eli was there.

I licked my lips, and looked up at him, and let out a breath.

"Eli."

"I could have lost you."

He moved forward then, cupped my face, and pressed his lips to mine.

If my own mistakes hadn't almost cost him everything, I would have been lost in that touch, in that kiss.

But I couldn't.

I couldn't let myself fall, not again. Not when my past had hurt his present and his future.

"You're okay. You're okay."

He kissed me again, then leaned back, studying my face. "I'm sorry it took me so long to get here, I had to talk with the cops, and then the firemen, and then my brothers, but finally, I'm here. Since you gave Kendall and Maddie permission for the doctors to speak to them, they told me that you were okay. Thank God."

"I'm okay. I'm so sorry, Eli. For everything."

He frowned. "Why are you sorry? It was Clint. Clint's the one that did all that."

"Clint's my ex-husband. I brought him here."

"You didn't make him do what he did. You have never been responsible for his choices. Even before that time he got down on his knee and proposed to you in a public setting, you were never responsible for anything that he did."

"And yet, I said yes to him. I said I would marry him. And then I left him. Something broke in him. I don't know what it was or why. But something changed."

"And I'm sure the authorities will figure that out, but none of that has anything to do with you."

"But I brought this all to you. You lost your building."

"Fuck that. It's just a building. We can rebuild. We have insurance."

"But I saw East. He looks like he saw a ghost."

I would never forget the way that Eli's brother had looked, looking at the fire, but Eli just squeezed my hand.

"East has gone through a lot of his own things and will continue to do so. Yes, seeing the fire and you being hurt brought some things back for him. It doesn't really change the way that he sees you."

"You can't know that." And what about how you see me?

But I didn't ask that.

"I hurt your business because of me. This is all me. My past, my ex-husband. If I had been smart and hadn't walked alone in the dark, this wouldn't have happened."

"Don't fucking blame yourself for that."

"It's hard not to. That's why I think the best thing for me to do is cut ties immediately and quit. I quit."

I hadn't realized I would say the words until they were already out, and even though it had felt like someone was ripping them from me, I knew they were for the best. The only things I needed to say. Because I was protecting Eli.

He just glared at me, his jaw clenched under his beard, his eyes shining.

"Fuck that."

"What?" I asked, surprised.

"I said fuck it. You don't get to quit."

"You don't get to tell me what to do," I snapped back, wondering why the hell we were fighting about this.

"No. It wasn't your fault what he did. You're the best thing that's happened to this company and the best thing that's ever fucking happened to me. You don't get to cut ties completely, to leave me, to leave the Wilders. You're one of us now. So get over it."

"Eli. This is going to be in the news, and it could hurt your reputation. It would be best if you could say I was no longer there."

"You can only leave if you want to, not because you think that you have to. And I see the way that you are with my family, with this company, with me. You are fucking amazing. So you don't get to leave. Do you understand me? You don't get to leave."

"You don't get to tell me what to do."

"Now, before your heart races and the nurses pull me out of here, I want you to understand something."

"What?" I asked, holding back tears. I needed to stop crying, but it was all just so much.

"I love you, Alexis Lane. I've loved you for longer than I care to admit. I fucking love you. I want you to work with me. Live with me. Plan our wedding. Fucking plan our future with me. Be part of this. I was thinking all of this before the fire, now that I almost lost you? No, I can't lose you again. I can't waste any more time. I saw you on that dance floor, that night over two years ago, I felt that connection then. And we have lost so much fucking time. I don't want to lose anymore, Alexis. Marry me. Be with me. But, whatever you do, don't leave me."

I let the tears fall this time, but there was no sadness there.

"I love you, too, Eli. But how? How did this happen?"

He laughed, and I joined him.

"I have no idea. One minute I was trying to figure out my life, the next minute a garter hit me in the chest, and you were catching a bouquet."

"I didn't mean to."

"I didn't mean to, either, but you plan everything else, so plan this. Plan who we are. But don't quit. Take a chance, but one that has a foundation. We, Wilders, need you, Alexis. I need you."

And when he kissed me again, I knew that there was a lot more to deal with, a lot more to worry about.

But in the end, I nodded yes, and kissed him back, knowing that he was my path. My future.

And no matter whatever happened with Clint, the authorities, and the Wilders, this was our inevitability.

I had made many choices to get where I was. In the end, there was only one way back to him.

And to us.

Chapter Twenty One

Eli

W ater slid down our backs as I pressed Alexis into the shower wall and knelt in front of her. She groaned, spreading herself for me, and I lapped at her, needing her taste.

In the months since the fire, since the attack, we had been careful with each other, oh so careful.

But now we didn't have to be.

I dug my fingers into her thighs, licking at her pussy and sucking at her clit as she came on my face. As soon as I stood up, she wrapped her arms around my neck, her breasts pressing against my chest. Her nipples were hard little points, so I pulled away from her mouth, sucking one nipple into my mouth, then the other, molding her breasts in my hands. She moaned, pressing her thighs together, so I slid my own thigh in between them, rubbing her cunt with my thigh.

"Eli. I need you."

"You've got me. Always."

I placed her on the bench that I had built in our custom shower, and slowly began to seat myself inside her, one thrust, then another. She wrapped her legs around my hips, and then we came together, meeting one another, pressing against one another.

And when I came, I groaned her name, biting at her lip, and she smiled against me, a gentle kiss, everything that I hadn't realized I needed.

Afterward, we showered quickly, trying not to take up all the hot water, and nearly ran into a box as we walked out, drying each other off.

"When do we get the new keys again?" she asked with a laugh.

I shook my head, smiling. "You know exactly when we close on our new house."

"True. I have it all in my planner. And Emily is ready to go to help me with the interior decorating part."

Emily was working full time now with Alexis, now

that the baby was a little bit older and able stay at home with Emily's wife.

That meant that Alexis had the exact amount of help she needed to work as many weddings at Wilder Resort and Winery as there were these days. Elliot had his own assistant with the other events, and I was somehow wrangling it all.

I wasn't quite sure, but we were making it work.

However, when the idea of where the two of us would live came about, we realized that a couple, a family, couldn't live in the apartment in the villa, nor could both of us fit comfortably in the small cabin.

So, for now, we were living at both and had bought a house near the resort.

Out of everything that had come from Alexis' past, her small inheritance from her grandmother helped secure her future so she wouldn't have to worry about leaning on former friends or an ex any longer. And she'd used part of it for the down payment for our home..

I was helping, of course, but this was what Alexis wanted to do.

Because I had given her a home when she first hadn't been able to make one, and then she was going to help me make our home.

"We do have too many boxes here."

"It's because all of the stuff that I got out of storage

doesn't actually fit in the cabin, so now it's here. And it's a little ridiculous."

"And then we get to move it all again to the house."

"It's not my fault that there was an actual tornado that hit the storage units and I nearly lost everything," she grumbled.

"Welcome to Texas, where tornadoes are fun."

"Okay, that's not a saying, don't make that a saying," she teased as we dressed quickly. I did my best not to watch her breasts bounce as she put on her bra. But it was very difficult.

"Because we decided to do a late shower after our meetings and some amazing shower gymnastics, we're running late for the family wine tasting."

"The new pour for the Wilders," I grumbled.

"Elijah and Evan are excited about this." She paused. "Okay, Elijah is excited about this. I'm not quite sure if Evan is."

"Evan isn't happy about a lot of things recently," I grumbled, and we both knew why. Not that we were actually talking to each other about it. Because if we said it out loud, then it made it real.

"Will Maddie be there?" she asked.

I shook my head. "No, she has a date?"

I hadn't meant say that so much like a question, but Alexis stumbled. "Seriously? How do I not know that?"

"Because I heard her mention it today in passing, and she was going to tell you and Kendall later. I swear to God I turned into a gossip magnet with this job, and I did not mean for that to happen."

"Oh wow. That's interesting."

"Yes. And a certain somebody knows as well, but none of us are talking about it because God forbid we do."

"I take it that means that Kendall's not coming then either?" she asked, and I rubbed my temple.

"No, the 'Days of Wilder Lives' is going to have to be put on hold while it's just family." The Wilder boys and upcoming Wilder girl.

She fluttered her eyelashes, my chest went tight in the best possible way, remembering that yes, I was marrying this woman soon. Fitting in our wedding at the Wilder Resort was going to be interesting. Mostly because I said I didn't care when or where we had the wedding, as long as it was us together, and she said that as a wedding planner, she was going to make sure we had the best wedding for us, and the Wilders needed to have it on the Wilder Resort. So, it was going to take a few months.

We made our way to the employee and family wine tasting area, and I nodded at a few people, spoke to a few guests, and did what I did best, apparently.

Made people feel comfortable. Which was a very odd thing considering I was a big man with a bigger beard, but people liked talking to me. And I fit right in.

Of course, I was nowhere near as good as Alexis, and when she slid her hand into mine and squeezed, I figured we made a good team.

The team that was going to help Wilder put a stamp on this part of Texas.

The guys were already there, snacking on cheese as they waited to open up the new bottles, and Alexis fit right in.

She went up to Elliot, hugged him tight, did the same with East, but his hug was slightly softer as if she was careful with him. I knew East understood why she was doing it, but he didn't push her away, and I had to count that as something.

She fist bumped with Elijah and Everett and then did a tiny little wave at Evan, who kept growling in the corner.

There was seriously something wrong with my brother, and I hoped to hell we figured out what it was soon.

"You're here. Now we can finally drink."

"Well, thank you. I love being invited," Alexis said with a laugh at Evan's growling words.

"Sorry, having a long day."

"It's okay. We're here for the wine. It's what you do best."

"I sure as fuck hope so," Evan growled.

Evan went through the motions with Elijah, going over the body and what grapes went into the wine. I honestly had no idea what they were talking about, but Alexis seemed interested.

"Maddie's better at this. We should have let her do it all," Evan grumbled, and Elijah stiffened only slightly before ignoring it, and we each took a sip of the wine. It was a robust pinot noir that settled over my tongue and tasted really damn good. I was starting to become pickier with my wines, and I thought that was a fricking magical feat considering I didn't even really know the difference between white and red wine before I moved here and opened up the winery. Oh yes, I knew a few things, and I could get my way around, but my brothers were best at it. And clearly, the Wilder wine genes hadn't gone to me.

We each took notes and then toasted, knowing that this was the wine that was going to go out to the next wine club, and what we'd be serving on our tours.

This felt like a future, like family.

"I see we're trying a new wine. How fun. May I have a glass?"

I turned at Dodge's voice as he and Brayden stood

there, glowering at us. No, Dodge was glowering. Brayden just looked smug. And I had a really bad fucking feeling about this.

"This is a private function. I'm sure you can join a tour that's about to start soon," Elijah said smoothly.

"Tour's not full? You can just add two people, kind of sad," Brayden added with a laugh, but Dodge shushed him.

"No need to gloat. About that."

"And when on earth do you want to gloat about?" Alexis asked with a sigh, and I squeezed her hand.

She had fought for herself so much recently, with Clint having gone to jail and having to deal with the press after the accident.

I didn't want her to have to deal with this.

"We just wanted to let you know that the Robin wedding will be heading to us. I'm sure they'll call you soon, but we wanted to make sure you heard about it from us. Face to face."

I froze as Alexis made a little noise that only I could hear, and I knew that was part of her heart breaking.

The Robin wedding was going to be *the* wedding of next year. With hundreds of guests from the social elite of Texas.

We had fought for it, and I thought we were going to get it, but it seemed we were wrong.

"It's all who you know and what Texas royalty sees. But, don't worry, I'm sure you can find a wedding or two for yourselves. What, marrying the help and all, you're going to have a wedding on the books that weekend probably, right?" Dodge added, and I stepped forward, but it was Alexis who pulled me back.

"Please give your staff all the best. The Robin wedding will be a lot of work, but if they trust you to do it well, I'm sure you will. Because I know if you fail that at all, all of the country elite here will know. Because they tell you with a smile that you're worthless and worth nothing. Because butter would never melt in your mouth."

"Don't worry. You don't have to threaten us."

"I'm not threatening you in the slightest."

"No, that's my job," I added, and both men glared at me.

Alexis just beamed. "Don't worry. You're going to give them the exact wedding they deserve, or you will get what you deserve. Am I right?" She giggled, and I held out my wine, my brother's following suit.

"Cheers. Now get the fuck out."

"You heard them. Go away now. Bye." Alexis added, her voice going high pitched.

"I'll make sure he gets out," Evan put in, but Amos,

the wine manager, walked in, looking big, bearded, and like he could hold a tank.

"Don't worry. I didn't realize that he was on the property. I'll make sure they find their way out. We don't want them to get lost. And nobody can ever hear them scream in the woods, right?" he added with a laugh, and both men growled before leaving on their own, leaving me standing there and looking down at Alexis.

"I'm sorry."

"No, it's okay. That was going to take all of my time and, frankly, while I wanted that wedding just to say that we could take it, it's going to be difficult. It's going to be one that if it's not perfect, the world, at least their world, will know it."

"I'm kind of glad we won't have the pressure."

I saw the sadness there, but only for an instant because then there was a gleam in her eye.

"And when they fail, and they will, because Dodge doesn't know what he's doing, we're going to be the ones that everyone comes to. Us, and Roy, of course.

"Hear hear. To Dodge failing, and us prospering." Elijah held up his glass, and I clinked mine to Alexis' before leaning down and taking her lips.

"To the Wilder future," she whispered.

"To you. Me. And everything Wild."

Mistakes were Made

Kendall

Sweat clung to me, as did a few other things I didn't want to think about, and I peeled a flour paste off my thigh.

"Well," a deep voice said from beside me, and I heaved out a breath, telling myself to focus. This wasn't the end of the world. I was fine. This was fine. Everything was fine.

And even in my head, the word *fine* kept going in higher and higher pitches, and I knew that indeed, it was anything but *fine*.

I stared at the ceiling, the gleaming metal bright and shiny.

The table beneath me buckled slightly but held

firm. I had to hope it would. Though considering every-thing we just did, it had seen worse.

The man next to me let out a deep breath, his chest shaking from exertion, and I knew he too was staring at that same damn ceiling.

Finally, I turned to my ex-husband, at his naked chest, ignoring my own nudity, at my breasts covered in flour and chocolate handprints, at my newly bruised hips, beard-burned-covered thighs, and ignored it all.

I looked at Evan Wilder, my ex-husband, and blinked.

He sat up, adjusting his prosthesis slightly. I didn't offer help him because I knew he'd hate it. I didn't do anything other than lay there, naked, bare to everything. He had seen everything anyway when we were younger, and I had been a little tighter, a little firmer. He saw everything now, and he had licked it and touched it and banged it against a table in my goddamned kitchen. Breaking every health code out in the world. We had done it all.

"What the fuck did we just do?" he asked, his voice rough. I did my best not to let it do anything to me. My body ached for him and from him, but my heart was rightfully encased in steal and ice.

I sat up and didn't bother covering myself. There was no need.

He wasn't doing it either. He looked down at my breasts, then at the thatch of hair between my legs. I looked down at his still semi-hard dick, then up at his face.

"It looks like we might have just done something that we're not going to talk about," I answered pointedly.

"Good, I guess we can just add it to the list."

And with that, I knew that I had just made yet another mistake when it came to Evan fucking Wilder.

Next in the Wilder Brothers Series:
Evan and Kendall figure out how to clean up
their mess in: Always the One for Me

IF YOU'D LIKE TO READ A BONUS SCENE FROM ELI
AND ALEXIS:
CHECK OUT THIS SPECIAL EPILOGUE!

A Note from Carrie Ann Ryan

Thank you so much for reading **One Way Back to Me.**

Writing a series set in my new home, surrounded by experiences I'm currently living (and dreaming up) is surreal and I'm having so much fun with the Wilder Brothers.

I'm already deep into the Wilder ways and I can't wait for you to read the rest of the brothers's stories. Starting with Evan and Kendall Always the One for Me. Oh boy...do they have a few things to work out!

If you'd like to read Eliza's story, you can find it in Inked Obsession!

The Wilder Brothers Series:

Next in the Wilder Brothers Series:
Evan and Kendall figure out how to clean up
their mess in: Always the One for Me

IF YOU'D LIKE TO READ A BONUS SCENE FROM ELI
AND ALEXIS:
CHECK OUT THIS SPECIAL EPILOGUE!

If you want to make sure you know what's coming next
from me, you can sign up for my newsletter at www.
CarrieAnnRyan.com; follow me on twitter at
@CarrieAnnRyan, or like my Facebook page. I also have
a Facebook Fan Club where we have trivia, chats, and
other goodies. You guys are the reason I get to do what I
do and I thank you.
Make sure you're signed up for my MAILING LIST so
you can know when the next releases are available as
well as find giveaways and FREE READS.
Happy Reading!

Also from Carrie Ann Ryan

The Montgomery Ink Legacy Series:

Book 1: Bittersweet Promises

The Wilder Brothers Series:

Book 1: One Way Back to Me

Book 2: Always the One for Me

Book 3: The Path to You

The Aspen Pack Series:

Book 1: Etched in Honor

The Montgomery Ink: Fort Collins Series:

Book 1: Inked Persuasion

Book 2: Inked Obsession

Book 3: Inked Devotion

Book 3.5: Nothing But Ink

Book 4: Inked Craving

Book 5: Inked Temptation

The Montgomery Ink: Boulder Series:

Book 1: Wrapped in Ink

Book 2: Sated in Ink

Book 3: Embraced in Ink

Book 3: Moments in Ink

Book 4: Seduced in Ink

Book 4.5: Captured in Ink

Book 4.7: Inked Fantasy

Book 4.8: A Very Montgomery Christmas

Montgomery Ink: Colorado Springs

Book 1: Fallen Ink

Book 2: Restless Ink

Book 2.5: Ashes to Ink

Book 3: Jagged Ink

Book 3.5: Ink by Numbers

Montgomery Ink Denver:

Book 0.5: Ink Inspired

Book 0.6: Ink Reunited

Book 1: Delicate Ink

Book 1.5: Forever Ink

Book 2: Tempting Boundaries

Book 3: Harder than Words

Book 3.5: Finally Found You

Book 4: Written in Ink

Book 4.5: Hidden Ink

Book 5: Ink Enduring

Book 6: Ink Exposed

Book 6.5: Adoring Ink

Book 6.6: Love, Honor, & Ink

Book 7: Inked Expressions

Book 7.3: Dropout

Book 7.5: Executive Ink

Book 8: Inked Memories

Book 8.5: Inked Nights

Book 8.7: Second Chance Ink

Book 8.5: Montgomery Midnight Kisses

Bonus: Inked Kingdom

The On My Own Series:

Book 0.5: My First Glance

Book 1: My One Night

Book 2: My Rebound

Book 3: My Next Play

Book 4: My Bad Decisions

The Promise Me Series:

Book 1: Forever Only Once

Book 2: From That Moment

Book 3: Far From Destined

Book 4: From Our First

The Less Than Series:

Book 1: Breathless With Her

Book 2: Reckless With You

Book 3: Shameless With Him

The Fractured Connections Series:

Book 1: Breaking Without You

Book 2: Shouldn't Have You

Book 3: Falling With You

Book 4: Taken With You

The Whiskey and Lies Series:

Book 1: Whiskey Secrets

Book 2: Whiskey Reveals

Book 3: Whiskey Undone

The Gallagher Brothers Series:

Book 1: Love Restored

Book 2: Passion Restored

Book 3: Hope Restored

The Ravenwood Coven Series:

Book 1: Dawn Unearthed

Book 2: Dusk Unveiled

Book 3: Evernight Unleashed

The Talon Pack:

Book 1: Tattered Loyalties

Book 2: An Alpha's Choice

Book 3: Mated in Mist

Book 4: Wolf Betrayed

Book 5: Fractured Silence

Book 6: Destiny Disgraced

Book 7: Eternal Mourning

Book 8: Strength Enduring

Book 9: Forever Broken

Book 10: Mated in Darkness

Book 11: Fated in Winter

Redwood Pack Series:

Book 1: An Alpha's Path

Book 2: A Taste for a Mate

Book 3: Trinity Bound

Book 3.5: A Night Away

Book 4: Enforcer's Redemption

Book 4.5: Blurred Expectations

Book 4.7: Forgiveness

Book 5: Shattered Emotions

Book 6: Hidden Destiny

Book 6.5: A Beta's Haven

Book 7: Fighting Fate

Book 7.5: Loving the Omega

Book 7.7: The Hunted Heart

Book 8: Wicked Wolf

The Elements of Five Series:

Book 1: From Breath and Ruin

Book 2: From Flame and Ash

Book 3: From Spirit and Binding

Book 4: From Shadow and Silence

Dante's Circle Series:

Book 1: Dust of My Wings

Book 2: Her Warriors' Three Wishes

Book 3: An Unlucky Moon

Book 3.5: His Choice

Book 4: Tangled Innocence

Book 5: Fierce Enchantment

Book 6: An Immortal's Song

Book 7: Prowled Darkness

Book 8: Dante's Circle Reborn

Holiday, Montana Series:

Book 1: Charmed Spirits

Book 2: Santa's Executive

Book 3: Finding Abigail

Book 4: Her Lucky Love

Book 5: Dreams of Ivory

The Branded Pack Series:
(Written with Alexandra Ivy)

Book 1: Stolen and Forgiven

Book 2: Abandoned and Unseen

Book 3: Buried and Shadowed

About the Author

Carrie Ann Ryan is the New York Times and USA Today bestselling author of contemporary, paranormal, and young adult romance. Her works include the Montgomery Ink, Redwood Pack, Fractured Connections, and Elements of Five series, which have sold over 3.0 million books worldwide. She started writing while in graduate school for her advanced degree in chemistry and hasn't stopped since. Carrie Ann has written over seventy-five novels and novellas with more in the works. When she's not losing herself in her emotional and action-packed worlds, she's reading as much as she can while wrangling her clowder of cats who have more followers than she does.

www.CarrieAnnRyan.com

Made in the USA
Las Vegas, NV
28 April 2022

48132443R00184